In the Grip of It

Also By Sheena Kamal

The Lost Ones
In the Grip of It (a novella)
It All Falls Down

In the Grip of It

of It

A Nora Watts Novella

SHEENA KAMAL

WITNESS
IMPULSE
An Imprint of HarperCollinsPublishers

Excerpt from *It All Falls Down* copyright © 2018 by Sheena Kamal.

Digital Edition MAY 2018 ISBN: 978-0-06-287932-5
Print Edition ISBN: 978-0-06-287933-2

Cover design by Amy Halperin
Cover photograph © rusm/ iStock/ Getty Images

WITNESS logo and WITNESS IMPULSE are trademarks of HarperCollins Publishers in the United States of America.

HarperCollins is a registered trademark of HarperCollins Publishers in the United States of America and other countries.

FIRST EDITION

18 19 20 21 22 OPM 10 9 8 7 6 5 4 3 2 1

For my mother

Chapter 1

THE MAN IS lying, has been lying all afternoon. I'm almost sure of it. I would be very sure if it wasn't for the over-the-counter painkillers I've been taking for the persistent ache in my shoulder, but we all have to make sacrifices to feel less pain in this world. I have given up some of my instinct for lies and Vikram Sharma has clearly forsaken the truth.

I have taken a ferry to get here, from Vancouver to Salt Spring Island, and have showed shown up unannounced among the blackberry bushes, looking for a spiritual-retreat-slash-working-farm-slash-racially-harmonious commune. The desire to call bullshit on this social experiment has been there since I stepped onto the grounds but, with great effort, I swallow the words. Everyone knows racial harmony doesn't exist.

"You know, our volunteers—potential new members

of our community, like yourself—are always surprised to discover how peacefully we live together on this part of the island," Vikram Sharma says. The one-man welcoming committee, Vikram is full of a brand of tranquility that most people associate with monks and that I associate with stoners. Tall and serene, with brown skin and dark hair that brushes his shoulders, he looks the part of a gatekeeper to peaceful living. He's giving me a tour of the main compound of this . . . whatever it is. "We have our own generators to use when the solar panels don't do the work. Our farm does well and we earmark a portion of our produce for our own consumption. We are vegans, so what little we need apart from what we grow is easily accessible at the grocery store. All in all, it is a fairly sustainable environment. Our harvests are quite fruitful."

"It sounds nice," I say, trying to look interested in veganism and sustainability. "Quite fruitful" is an understatement for Spring Love, one of the most prosperous farms on Salt Spring Island. Despite Vikram's lies, from what I've seen so far, it does seem like that elusive thing that people the world over come to the west coast in search of: a happy place full of nature and organic produce.

The midday heat sits heavily on us, the way it only seems to do during the month of August. Vikram is handling it a lot better than me. He doesn't look as if he could perspire, even if he wanted to, whereas I'm covered in a fine sheen of sweat that has been slicked to my body since this morning.

"Oh, it is nice. Working together to plant and harvest and feed our people has been the delight of my life. I've been here for five years now and I don't think I could live any other way. The only thing we ask of people who come to join our lifestyle, or even just to try it out, is to relinquish their connection to the digital world while they're here. So that they can fully immerse themselves in the experience. Unplug. We usually make that clear to volunteers before they get here, the ones that call first, that is."

This is a not-so-subtle rebuke, but I don't mind. The reason I didn't call first is because I didn't want to take the chance they'd say no. "You want my cell phone?"

He laughs and I'm almost certain the laughter is real. I wonder just what it will take to ruffle this man, whose soulful brown eyes remind me of a golden retriever. It's possible that I'm missing my dog Whisper but I know she's doing okay back in Vancouver, safe and complaining about the heat in the way that she does. With her mournful stares and silent demands for ice cubes in her water bowl.

"Yes, we want your cell phone, your laptop, your personal reading device and your video-game console. You can leave at any time, but if you want to stay with us awhile, you'll be trapped here without Big Brother looking over your shoulder."

It's clear he's expecting me to join in the laughter, so I do, but I'm not a good actor and I wonder if I'm fooling anybody.

Haha, yes. I definitely want to join a commune on Salt Spring Island, the hippiest of the hippy Gulf Islands. Who wouldn't?

When I hand over my phone, Vikram leads me to the women's quarters, off the main building. On our way there we pass the schoolhouse, where, through the open door, I see a handful of children varying in age and shades of brown sitting at long tables, working independently of one another. For a moment I zero in on one, a boy about ten years old, with dark skin and a little afro, but am careful to move on quickly.

Vikram notices my interest, though. "That's the camp for the kids. We have a supervised afternoon program for them. One of our members here, Shoshanna, is a teacher. Do you have children of your own?"

"Yes, a teenage daughter. She lives in Toronto now." I'm careful to keep my tone even, but Vikram is perceptive. He puts a hand on my shoulder. Reflexively, I shake it off. Some habits die hard, even when you're trying to convince someone—and even maybe yourself—that you genuinely want to be part of this island love fest.

He notices the gesture but doesn't apologize for it. Then he continues as though it never happened. "It's a shame about your daughter. Parents should never be separated from their children. It's an aberration of modern society, one that disturbs the natural order of community. It takes a village to raise a child and children to lift their villages up, spiritually. This is something we strongly believe in here at Spring Love. Healing through the power of community." There's something in his voice that I don't like, something hard beneath his dulcet tones. The golden retriever turns pit bull for a fraction of a moment, then he's back to looking at me with his big brown eyes.

In the women's quarters, he shows me to a small room with a bed, a closet, and a dresser. "Bathroom facilities are at the end of the hall. After you get settled you can help out in the kitchen for the evening meal. Oh yes, I can see you're surprised. We all pitch in for meals, even on our first day. It's part of what makes it so special. I think you'll be very happy here, Nora. I really do," he says, lying again.

"I was hoping to get started on the farm."

"I'm sorry, we're full up with the farm these days, but need a hand in the kitchen. Don't worry, spaces open up quickly."

He's only shown me a fraction of the grounds, which I know contain fields for harvesting crops, living quarters, a retreat center, and private yurts for families. Before Vikram goes, he takes my cell phone. "Aren't you tired of it all, Nora? All this documenting life without actually living it. These digital tethers that drag us down? You did the right thing coming to us. I can see you need our help, and to help people throw off the shackles of capitalism is why we're here. You can rest assured we *will* help you."

"Throwing off the shackles of capitalism is exactly why I'm here. Thank you for agreeing to let me be a part of your community." I smile through this absurdity, though it feels strange and wrong. I am here because of capitalism, but because the shackles are firmly on—and will stay that way until I get what I came for. Everyone's gotta eat.

Vikram smiles back. On the surface we seem to be in perfect agreement, but the thing is, he doesn't think I'll be happy here at all.

I've not fooled him and he hasn't fooled me. We both know that I'm not here to be part of their so-called harmonious society. I have an ulterior motive and he wants to know what it is before he shows me to the edge of the property and, hopefully, gives me back my phone. So I guess I have to work quickly to get what I came here for.

Without the phone, though, I'm left with no way to communicate with the people who sent me to Spring Love in the first place.

Chapter 2

LAST WEEK A man came into our PI office, looked around the shabby interior, frowned, and said, "I must have gotten the address wrong."

"Depends," I replied. "What are you looking for?"

"An investigator."

"Nope, you're in the right place," I said, looking at his nice suit, shiny shoes, and expensive watch.

"Are you sure? Maybe I should come back later."

He was clearly trying to make a graceful exit. Before the man could leave, I got up from behind my desk and opened the door to Leo Krushnik's office. "Leo, there's someone here to see you."

"Well," said the man, who was hesitating behind me, "I'm not really sure that this is the right fit for me." He was trying to be diplomatic about the condition of our office and what it might say about his own level of desperation that he was here, but we weren't about to let a potential client go without a fight. His level of desperation was no match for ours.

Leo Krushnik, the head of our little operation, walked around his desk and beamed at the man. "We're the right fit for anybody," he said, grasping the man's hand and giving it a firm shake. "We prefer to keep our overhead low so that we can offer competitive rates to people who need our services, regardless of their personal incomes. Please, have a seat."

The man sat, a little overwhelmed by Leo's charm, which is considerable. That day Leo was dressed in linen pants and a simple cotton shirt, as a nod to the heat wave the city was experiencing. He could pull off this look as easily as he pulled off the lie about our rates. We keep our overhead low because this dump on Hastings Street, in the derelict Downtown Eastside of Vancouver, is all we can afford, but clients didn't need to know that. And even I could admit that the "competitive rates" line sounded good—even true—coming from Leo.

"How can I help you?" Leo asked.

"My name is Ken Barnes, and I'm concerned about my son, Trevor. My ex-wife Cheyenne moved to Salt Spring last year with Trevor and I think she's gotten into some kind of trouble there. She won't bring him back to Vancouver and visitation has been difficult."

Leo frowned. "Because they're on an island?" Salt Spring wouldn't be easy to ferry to and from on a regular basis.

"Yes, but that's not the only reason. She keeps putting off my visits and it's been difficult to arrange for Trevor to come into Vancouver. I think . . . I think she's in some kind of cult, to be honest. They call it a commune, but you know those stories about Bountiful?"

"Yes," said Leo. Everyone knew the stories about Bountiful, British Columbia, where fundamentalist polygamous communities live and proliferate seemingly freely.

"Well, I think it's something like that. Cheyenne wants to be in some kind of crazy sex cult, sure. She's not my wife anymore and I really don't care what she does. But I'm fighting for custody of Trevor. I want him out of there."

"And you need some ammo." Leo looks up from his pad, where he's been taking notes. "You've come to the right place, Ken. We've done surveillance work for many child-custody cases." Another lie, but Ken didn't notice. We'd only done a handful of those, but "many" is relative. "You understand that this won't be cheap? We'll have to get out to the island and spend some time gathering information."

"That's fine. There's nothing I won't pay to get my son out of there. Cheyenne, she . . . well, she struggled with depression and anxiety for years and she let a lot of toxic people into her life who fed on her struggles. It was like a sick downward spiral. When she started doing yoga and got certified as a teacher, I thought she'd changed. But I'm not sure anymore. I know this sounds terrible—I know it does—but I don't trust her judgment about the people she lets into her life. Especially men."

"She married you," Leo said.

"I know, but this is the thing: it's not about me and her anymore. We're done. This is about Trevor—and me doing my part as a father, making sure he's safe. That he has a good life. I just want results."

"We can't guarantee results." This is the first time I'd spoken since the initial exchange. Ken Barnes's startled gaze meets mine. He'd clearly forgotten I was there, which was not unusual. "Maybe it is a sex cult, maybe it isn't. All we can do is take a look and document what we find."

"I know that nothing is certain, but I know my son deserves a healthy, *normal* life. Whatever they're doing on that island is not normal. It just isn't. It's one step away from homeschooling, and who's to say they're not making him do hard labor?"

What is normal, anyway? I didn't ask Barnes for clarification. I just kept silent as Leo agreed to take his money in exchange for the work. Before he let Barnes go, he pulled him aside. "Nora's right, Ken, about any sort of guarantee. But what I *can* say is that if there's something to find, chances are we will get a sense of it."

In the next few days, I started the file on Cheyenne Barnes and looked through the information Ken had provided us. "Cheyenne scrubbed her social-media profiles last year," he explained to me, over the phone. "I thought she was punishing me by erasing the memories and keeping me away from what's happening with my son, but now that I think about it, there's something fishy about this whole thing." So he kept saying.

Cheyenne is smiling in all the photos, and in every single one there is something wistful about her, a faraway look in her eyes. Something that suggests a romantic nature. She's an instructor for hot yoga, which I thought was stretching for attractive people but later discovered is actually sweaty stretching. Who knew. She'd gone to Salt Spring Island two years ago to work at a yoga retreat and, according to Ken, never came back. She met a man there, a fellow yoga enthusiast, and rebuffed all of Ken's attempts at reconciliation.

There is very little to be found on Cheyenne Barnes's new man. He has no social-media profiles of his own, but I did find a picture of him on the Spring Love website. Some people are so attractive it's almost surreal, and Vikram Sharma is one of them.

Chapter 3

DURING MEAL PREPARATION, I try to do a better job of seeming like I'm in need of peace and tranquility. It's not a stretch. This past winter I had gone on a search to find my missing daughter Bonnie, a girl I'd given up for adoption as soon as she was born. During the search I got shot in the shoulder, hurt my ankle, almost drowned, and was possibly saved by a whale. If anyone can use some healing, it's me.

That's what Leo thinks, anyway.

He is too polite to bring up that my work at our little PI agency has been slower than normal because of my slack, which isn't entirely my fault, though I feel guilty about it anyway. I've graduated from secretary and unofficial apprentice to secretary and official apprentice, working with him to get the hours necessary to be licensed on my own, but it is taking a while to get back into my usual groove. That's why, when Ken Barnes showed up, Leo insisted I take the case. A simple surveillance assignment, he told me. Take good notes. Relax a little, he said, somewhat tensely.

I told him about my hatred of ferries, but he just laughed that off. "What are you talking about? Everyone loves going to the Gulf Islands! Don't worry, Nora. You just have to take two little ferries, I promise. One to the island and one from it. This job pays well, too, and Sebastian and I have a little staycation planned ourselves. So this will be good for all of us. You'll free me up, and get to spend some time on the island, with expenses and half the fee. Plus, we'll look after Whisper while you're away. What do you say?"

I said yes, of course, because Seb, Leo's partner, has been looking exhausted lately. His freelance commissions have been up, but it has taken a toll on his health. Seb and Leo have been sniping at each other lately, and I agree, a vacation would be good for them. And I could use the money. The only unhappy party in all this is my dog, Whisper, who loves Seb and Leo but has been stuck to me ever since my near drowning. When I left for the ferry this time, I could hear her barking at me as I walked away. Insisting I come back.

"She'll be fine," Seb assured me. "I know this is work, but try to enjoy yourself a little, Nora."

"Yeah, you too."

Seb turned away. Funny, that. Sebastian Crow, the journalist I have spent the past few years working with, somehow couldn't meet my eyes. He ran a hand through his hair, which looked dull and flat. Seb has never cared much about his appearance, but he'd never looked worse. I'm not in much of a position to judge, then or now, but I couldn't help but notice.

But that's all in my past.

In my immediate future there are vegetables to be chopped for green smoothies and a big, hearty salad, while a huge pot of vegetarian chili simmers on the stove. Vikram has been in and out of the kitchen but has left me with the cook, Kelly, who speaks in monosyllables and gives me tasks any idiot could do, which is an accurate assessment of my cooking skills.

A battered black pickup truck pulls in behind the kitchen and two women get out. One unloads reusable grocery bags from the truck while the other disappears somewhere further into the compound. With Kelly's blessing, I abandon the vegetables to help with the groceries.

"Thanks. I'm Cheyenne," says the woman unloading groceries with me. She pushes her braids off her face. Her features remind me of the boy in the schoolhouse, but I already knew she was his mother. "You must be Nora. Vik called ahead to let us know that you showed up to volunteer."

Cheyenne washes her hands at the sink, dries them, and offers me one. I shake it.

"Nice grip you got there, Nora. Vik didn't tell me that."

"We didn't shake hands."

She glances down. "You have working hands—that's good. We get a lot of yoga types this way, who've never done a full day's work in their lives. But I get the feeling you know what hard labor is. That's the kind of woman we need at this farm, to be honest, though we'd never turn anyone away. As long as you're willing to work, you've got a place here. Roof over your head and food in your belly. A place to quiet your mind."

"That's what I'm looking for."

She grins. "Good. This is where you'll find it. After dinner, come to the fire pit with us. We do a nightly circle, for those who want some company.

Dinner is buffet style and not well attended. The children have all eaten by the time I get a plate. A handful of hippies trickles through, casting curious glances my way. But nobody attempts conversation. Cheyenne and Vikram are the only people who join me, and I get the sense that this is by design. The woman who'd slipped away after leaving Cheyenne with the groceries returns. She has neat dreads to her shoulders and a suspicious look in her eye whenever she looks in my direction. For a moment I think she's going to come sit with us, but she takes a seat several tables away and begins reading through files as she eats.

Cheyenne notices my interest in her. "Have you met Wanda?"

"No. I saw her come in with you earlier, though."

"She's the GM of this place," Vikram informs me.

"Does all the admin work and posts the schedules. She's also my ex-wife." Seeing my surprise, he laughs, which is starting to get on my nerves. All this innocent laughter for my benefit.

"If it works for you all," I say.

Cheyenne kisses Vikram on the cheek. "Oh, it does. Vikram and Wanda have known each other since they were kids, but their marriage didn't work because they were never more than friends."

"It's nothing like what me and Cheyenne have. That's why we're getting married this fall. I'm with the woman of my dreams."

By the way she's deliberately ignoring us all, I can tell the woman of his past has heard everything. She keeps her head down, but her spoon pauses midway to her mouth. Then she continues eating, as though nothing has happened.

Vikram continues the verbal gymnastics from earlier. He elaborates and manufactures. Cheyenne sits there and nods. She believes Vikram, every word, and that is a testament to the power of love, because the only thing that is true about this story is that she might be the woman of his dreams. Everything else that comes out of his mouth is a lie.

Cheyenne is unperturbed at the lies, or maybe love has blinded her to them. Maybe it's because I'm a little numb myself, so I don't pay them too much attention. I wait a polite enough amount of time before I excuse myself. "You'll be at circle tonight, won't you?" Cheyenne asks.

"At the fire pit, right?"

"Yup!" Vikram beams at me. "We'll see you soon!"

In the women's quarters I walk down the hall, checking rooms as quietly as I can. There are no locks here. As far as I can tell, of the six rooms in this section, only three are occupied. And that's including my own. This confirms what I saw in the dining room, too. In the height of the summer, this place is all but empty. I pause in the doorway of my own room and feel, instinctively, that something is wrong. Someone has been in here while I was busy in the kitchen, living the vegan life. Nothing has been taken from my backpack, but someone has clearly been through it, leaving behind a few strands of dark hair on the ground beside my things.

About an hour later, gathered loosely around a fire pit with a half dozen hippies and a few children, I look over at Wanda. She looks right back at me, not tearing her gaze away or backing down. I remember watching her enter the women's quarters from the back window of the kitchen and come back out twenty minutes later. From what I saw, no one else went in there. Despite what the happy couple Vikram and Cheyenne think, Wanda doesn't seem as settled as everyone else. As happy, either.

There's a beat-up old Gibson nearby, and with Vikram's nod of approval, I pick it up and begin to tune it by ear. The Gibson feels good in my hands, and is still a nice instrument. The people around the fire begin to relax at my handling of the guitar. They want to hear me play, but only the children let themselves enjoy it when I start to strum idly. It's possible they want me to play something corny, some happy kumbaya song, but I refuse on principle. I start playing Sister Rosetta Tharpe's *"Rock Me,"* because there was always a kind of joy to her music.

The kids, they clap and dance, forgetting they've been told not to trust strangers like me, because nobody ever told them that a stranger with a guitar is the most dangerous kind around. Kids can say no to candy or junk food of any variety if they're taught to respect the warning signs. But a guitar on a cool summer evening? When the salty ocean breeze passes through the trees and lifts your hair and your spirits to the sky? Nobody can resist that.

The human species has evolved to want music, to crave that connection with the things you can feel in your soul. And I'm okay with a guitar. More than okay, even though it's been a while since I've picked one up. If you have an ear for it, it's one of those things you can't lose even if you tried.

I play a little from *"Can't Help Falling in Love,"* because I was warned this could be a sex cult, and love songs seem more appropriate than the blues I prefer. Then I set the guitar aside because mostly everyone is gone. Someone's come around with hot cocoa, and it's cool enough out that the thick, bitter chocolate feels good going down my throat. There's some clapping, some loosening of the group's attitude toward me, so much that Cheyenne doesn't notice when her son, Trevor, the little boy I'd seen in the schoolhouse, slips from her side and edges toward me. "How do you do that?" he asks, looking at the Gibson.

"Let me show you." I position the guitar in his hands, which are small but surprisingly strong. I can feel Cheyenne from across the fire, as she comes alert. So, very carefully, I show Trevor how to play the first part of "Can't Help Falling In Love." He's a quick learner.

Cheyenne finds her way to our side of the fire. While her son gets used to the guitar, she smiles at me. There's something indefinable in her gaze, something maybe a little sad. "Put an instrument in a black kid's hand, or a basketball, and that's all the world will ever see of him."

"He might be good," I say, nodding to the guitar. "He might like it."

"He might be good and he might like it, but sometimes that's all people will see. Maybe he's got more in him than that."

More in him than the gift of music? Whoever wanted anything better than that? I understand her position, but I've never had much to recommend me but my musical ability. Maybe Trevor has something better to offer the world. Cheyenne thinks so, at least.

"Trevor," Vikram calls, from the path. "Time for bed, buddy."

Something flashes in Trevor's expression, just a flicker of heat, then it's gone. Trevor puts the guitar down and joins Vikram. There's an unmistakable tension in him as Vikram squeezes his shoulder. It was the same reaction I had when Vikram put his hand on my shoulder earlier. A friendly gesture, but an unwelcome one. I don't know what Trevor's reaction is about, but I know I don't like it.

Ken Barnes was right. There is something strange here.

"You ever been here before? To Salt Spring?"

With great difficulty I pull my attention back to Cheyenne, as Vikram and Trevor disappear up the path. "No. First time."

"Ah. You may not know, then, that this was a place of refuge for the black community fleeing oppression and discrimination in California. They came here and to Vancouver Island, too."

"I didn't know that."

"People think it's all retirees and hippies—well, there's lots of them, too. But black folks have had roots here going back to the mid-eighteen hundreds. A long time ago my family on my mother's side made a home in Victoria, but I like Salt Spring better. I'm hoping it will be a home for Trevor. His dad's a big-shot lawyer, but I don't want that life for Trev. It can be if he wants it, later on, but I think kids these days need to know what a simple life can be. A place like this, they can learn to be happy with themselves. That's a kind of skill that many people these days don't have. His dad certainly doesn't have it."

"But Vikram does," I say.

"Vikram is a master at it. It's part of the reason I love him so much. He is who he is. He cares about being happy, being at peace."

"Right," I say, wanting to point out that we are all who we are, because that's how life works.

Movement catches my eye near the kitchen, which is just barely in view. A group of six people, by my count, leaves through the back entrance, lit by the single outdoor bulb over the door. Where did they come from? None of them look our way and the hippies at the fire don't look over at them. It's as though they don't even exist. What kind of harmonious living is this?

"Finish your cocoa," Cheyenne says. "And I'll walk you back to your room."

"I'm done." I pour the rest of the cocoa into the fire, about half the mug, and turn to Cheyenne. "Where do you stay?"

"In private quarters with Vikram and Trev. But don't worry, you won't be alone. Wanda and Shoshanna, our schoolteacher, will be there to keep a look out for you. Tomorrow I'll show you the yoga retreat. We're having a session there in a couple days, but for now it's free."

About half an hour later, in a small but surprisingly comfortable single bed, I lay awake with the curtains open. It doesn't matter that anyone passing by can see me in bed, fully clothed. What does matter is that I'm suddenly lightheaded and feeling nauseous. I try to ignore it by thinking about why Vikram and Cheyenne felt they needed to hide a group of brown people entering the kitchen hours after everyone else had eaten, and why the other hippies around the fire did not give a flying fuck.

Chapter 4

THE FEELING OF nausea persists. Living as a vegan clearly isn't for me. Something I ate isn't sitting right, and the lightheadedness just won't go away. I'm shivering now, so I put on a dark blue jean jacket with a happy-face button pinned to it. The jacket isn't mine. I borrowed it from Stevie Warsame, Leo's surveillance guy, because somebody from somewhere once left it behind in his car and it had offended his personal sense of style. But it's the perfect disguise for somebody trying to join a commune and, according to Leo, looks cute when you put some buttons on it.

I feel terrible, but I get the sense I might be kicked out of Spring Love sooner rather than later, so I force myself to get moving before dawn. I'm hoping everyone has fallen into their REM cycles, as nature intended. That's the only explanation I have for the complete freedom I feel walking through the corridor of the women's quarters, around the schoolhouse, past the fire pit, and down toward the fields. The narrow path I noted during my tour with Vikram is still as isolated as ever, snaking through the trees, so that the fieldwork happens out of sight. Again, this doesn't seem all that harmonious to me, but I must have different standards.

It should feel nice, being out in the cool night, feeling the summer breeze tickling the hair at the nape of my neck. I should feel better than I do, but I am strangely unsteady on my feet and I can't help but let my thoughts wander. Here in the dark, on this path, I long for the city. I live in the basement of the office on Hastings, and there's always something happening out on that street. When it's not the sound of people moving about, car engines starting, the wailing of fire trucks and ambulances, it's the whispers of poverty that I hear. Hushed voices of people huddled together. The slide of bodies in sleeping bags. The quiet sobs. The drug-addled moans of euphoria, then, on its heels, despair. These are the sounds of my city at night, and I miss them so much right now. I can't remember the last time I felt so alone and I hate myself for the thought. I also can't remember the last time I allowed myself to think like this.

I focus instead on the moon, which seems bigger and brighter than it should be now that morning is almost upon me. Am I going insane?

The path opens suddenly and there in front of me are the fields. There's a building to my right, a kind of refurbished barn. A single light is on inside. A toilet flushes. Moments later, the light goes out and the building goes dark. I wait a few moments, feeling an odd sense of panic, then shake it off and move toward the building. It doesn't look like the photos of the yoga retreat I saw online. There are few windows and the ones I see are high up on the second floor.

The door closest to me is locked, so I skirt around to the door on the opposite side of the building. That one is locked as well. But just a few feet away, a window is open. Just a bit, but it's enough for me to lift it up the rest of the way. A glance inside tells me this is a bathroom, hence the window, and somebody has been careless. Or maybe leaving this window cracked was deliberate.

Somebody approaches from the trees off to the side, not the path, but I have no time to duck or hide or pull myself through the window and into the building.

There's a moment of surprise and a teenage girl materializes in front of me. Her build is slight, though she's quite tall. Taller than me, anyway. We stare at each other for a moment. The girl's expression is startled, then becomes terrified. I hear a footstep behind me and am about to turn when the girl lashes out with a fist, the contact inexpertly light. But that doesn't hide the fact that any strike to the eye hurts like hell. There's a moment of blindness, then a streak of red beneath the lid. I don't know what to do. I'm not one to shrug off a blow, but I hesitate because something about this girl's features reminds me of my daughter Bonnie. Of the photographs I'd seen of her. She would be around this girl's age. Why am I even thinking about this now?

This moment, barely a split second, takes the momentum out of me.

I feel arms come around me from behind and grab my shoulders. I kick out behind me and there's a pained cry as my foot connects with a knee. It's a male voice, but belongs to neither a child nor a man. Someone in between, maybe the same age as the girl who hit me. The arms behind me slip, but a hand digs for purchase into my shoulder. Pain sears through me and I stumble.

The door behind me opens and, in the breaking light of the dawn, I count four more faces as they descend toward me.

There are questions spoken in languages I don't understand. The hand still presses into my shoulder and the pain is too great to be believed, even by me. And I've felt enough physical pain in my lifetime to know. I'm grabbed and hauled into the building. Are they trying to help me? I try another kick but find no purchase, only managing to upset everyone's balance and knock my own head into a wall. I don't see stars, but I see faces, triple the number I'd seen outside the building when they picked me up. I remember, far too late, that I haven't taken any painkillers since the ferry ride over here. Someone's hands falter and I'm dropped to the ground. With a surge of strength that surprises even me, I stand and stumble toward the open door in front of me.

But it's not the exit, as I imagined. I fall halfway down a set of stairs, and realize that I'm in a basement. In the dark. Hearing the bolt slide on the door I've just barreled through.

Chapter 5

I DON'T KNOW what's wrong with me, but it feels like I'm dying of thirst. It's been a few minutes or several hours, I can't tell. I force myself to start paying attention. A woman hums quietly on the other side of the door. Another person hushes her, but forty-eight seconds later she starts again. The pain in my shoulder is starting to recede, but I can't help blaming myself for it anyway because it's really my fault I got shot there in the first place. I assume it's my fault because, although I don't remember getting shot, if there's one thing I've learned about myself over the years it's that I'm not a woman who takes a bullet by accident.

Also my fault is that I allowed myself to be distracted by the teenage girl who used my hesitation to punch me in the face. This would never have happened a year ago. My reflexes were better then. But just a few months back, Bonnie had gone missing. She'd been adopted almost as soon as she was born and I was not part of her life until very recently. Jury's out as to whether I'm part of her life now. I've begun to think about her again and this madness has put her at the forefront of my mind. So much that I let myself be distracted when facing another teenage girl, one with a decent right cross. If I hadn't been on the receiving end of it, I might have even been impressed.

Every now and then footsteps pass over me and, if I listen carefully, I can hear people talking in the hall. What I can hear of the whispers is that most of them are in accented English. The accents aren't the same, though, which makes me think that English isn't everyone's first language but it is the common one. Also common is the subject matter—namely, me.

I'm able to pick up snippets of hushed conversation.

"Cop—" says a woman. Something in her voice is familiar. She must be the woman who couldn't stop humming.

"They call them RCMP here—" says a young man.

A young woman snorts. "Not all of them are RCMP."

"I'm not RCMP," I say loudly, through the space at the bottom of the door. "Not any other kind of cop, either. Can I get some water?"

"Shut up," another person says. Someone new.

I lose track of the speakers for a moment, as they begin to argue.

"You can't tell a police officer to shut up."

"But she just said she wasn't a police officer!"

"Use your brain! That's exactly what police would say."

"She didn't look like police to me."

My head spins and, for a moment, it feels like I'm on a boat. I clear my throat and try again. "Because I'm not." I realize why my captors have been nice enough to let me listen in on their conversations. It's because they don't know what they're doing.

Beneath the thrum of whispers, there's another sound. Footsteps coming into the building. Then a cool voice cuts through. "Shut up right now, all of you. Get back to your rooms."

"But what do we do with her?"

I don't hear the response. Several walk away, one, quite literally, dragging his feet. I think of the boy—no, the young man—whose knee I kicked in the struggle.

I'm feeling angry, and wish I'd kicked his knee harder. But he's just a kid, really, and I'd clearly surprised him and his girlfriend as they were sneaking back into the building. It's hard to blame young love, so I guess I'm back to blaming myself for being stupid enough to get caught like this. I'm glad, in a way, that I have. Because aside from Ken Barnes's fears and suspicions, I now know for a fact that something is deeply wrong here at Spring Love. I have to wonder why they shut me in here in the first place. Why the building itself has been locked down. Why those kids felt the need to sneak away to be together. If this really was a racially harmonious sex cult, would they not just let those teenagers be?

I think back to a few moments before everyone left, and what I heard. I am good with voices, better than good. It's maybe because I was once a blues singer, because the words don't mean as much as the voice beneath them. What the voice is truly saying. And that no matter what tone, what context I hear a voice in, it's always immediately recognizable to me, in all its forms.

What I heard was Vikram Sharma come in and tell my confused kidnappers to get back to sleep. He sounded different. Cold. Calculated. The warmth was gone because he wasn't lying.

Someone approaches. No, more than one person. There's a sense that I'm being considered, weighed, evaluated. The smell of vanilla coming through the bottom of the door is a sudden onslaught to my senses.

I hear Vikram say ". . . Can't afford to take the chance . . ."

Then Cheyenne, I think, chimes in: ". . . not sure she's a cop." There's true remorse in her voice. She seems sad. Well I'm sad, too. I didn't want it to be a sex cult but, right now, I think I would take a bunch of perverts over whatever the hell I've found here, which suddenly seems much, much worse.

"Water, please," I say, speaking through the bottom of the door.

There's a pause. Some more consideration of me, perhaps.

They walk away, but the smell of vanilla lingers. I stop paying attention again, hit by another wave of nausea. I close my eyes for a second and when I open them, I'm too late to catch the door opening. A small bottle is shoved through, but it isn't water. When I unscrew the cap, I find some of the green smoothie from dinner. It's chilled, at least, feels good going down my throat.

For a few minutes, I feel better. But my head is still swimming. My mind wanders.

I have been thinking about my future recently. When I first went back to work, Seb and Leo (who share office space) exchanged concerned glances and told me they thought I should consider a less-dangerous business. After what I'd been through looking for my birth daughter, knowing that PI work can be boring but isn't exactly danger free, they thought there could be something else for me.

So what did I do?

I doubled down.

"I want my license," I said to Leo, who, along with our surveillance guy, Stevie Warsame, is a licensed PI. You have to be, to work in Vancouver. Leo was unhappy about me continuing in this line of work, but he eventually relented. I'm too valuable an employee to lose, anyway. But I had to start putting in the hours, officially, even though I'd unofficially been doing this work for a couple years now. Stevie Warsame refused to help train me because of my unpredictable nature and my habit of looking at him as though he's lying, which he doesn't do very often, and when he does it's only about mundane things like where he buys his clothes.

Thinking back on it, of course I should have listened to reason.

I'm in a cellar, though for some reason it feels as though I'm on a boat. There are no windows here and the light switch is on the other side of the door. There's no lock on the doorknob, or above it either, which means the door is bolted shut from the outside. I go down thirteen steps and feel my way around the space. The darkness is almost as oppressive as the heat I've been complaining about all summer, but I'd take the sun any day if it means getting out of this place. On the opposite side of the room is a set of stone steps leading up to another door. I'm guessing, to the exterior of the building.

That's as far as I get.

I don't get sick immediately, but when I do, it hits me hard. It's like the worst cramps I've ever had, multiplied by a thousand. I'm sweating, with my face pressed into the wall. My heart is beating fast and I can hear sounds in the darkness—terrible, awful scratching sounds. As though there are rats all around. It feels as though I've been taken by some kind of madness, that I'm in the grip of it. A light appears on the other side of the room, at the top of the stone steps. Someone has thrown open the cellar doors. I make it up the stairs and outside into the morning light.

"Oh my God. How did you manage to lock yourself in the cellar?" asks Wanda, out of nowhere. She walks toward me, concern writ plain on her face. "Were you taking a peek, and someone accidentally locked the door on you?"

"I need a doctor," I say.

"Don't worry. I'm going to get you some help."

Thank God. I'm half dragged, half carried to the pickup truck, which is conveniently close by. Was it on the path when I came down here? Wanda squeezes my hand as she helps me into the truck. What else am I supposed to do? I can't stop staring at the moon, hoping it will ground me somehow. It should be fading in the dim morning light, but is perversely still around to confuse me. Why is it still so bright? I decide I am going insane.

Wanda drives me to the emergency department of the island's tiny hospital, where she immediately takes charge. "Her name is Nora Watts and she just came to us yesterday. I found her in our cellar. I think she ate some poisonous mushrooms, got sick, and fell down the stairs."

"No," I say. My face feels red, then pink and blue. My face feels colors, even though that's absurd, and yet it makes perfect sense.

"It might be too late to pump her stomach," says the doctor. I hate his face. I hate that he believes her. "We sometimes use benzodiazepines for sedation but she might be here for the drugs."

"She might," says Wanda. "We do get those types every now and then."

"She's lying," I gasp.

"Oh, sweetie, why didn't you come to us when you started feeling sick?" Wanda asks. Why is she still here? "We would have brought you here right away."

Out of the corner of my eye I see Wanda take the doctor aside. "We get these drugged-out types every now and then, looking to volunteer with us. I found some pills in her bag—"

Which she hands to the hovering nurse.

"Painkillers. Have a prescription. My shoulder," I say. But nobody listens.

"Will do, Wanda. Thanks for bringing her in. This happens all the time. There was a man that came in a few months ago with ayahuasca in his system."

Another debilitating attack of cramps takes my attention, but not before I notice Wanda's slight hesitation. "God, yes, I heard it at the farmer's market. Crazy."

Then the attention is back on me. "Do you know what mushrooms she ate?"

"If it is mushrooms at all—that's just a guess on my part. But you know we leave the dedicated forest spaces on our property alone. She was free to wander about. We only had her helping out with dinner prep but didn't see much of her after that. She may have even brought the mushrooms with her. Usually it's marijuana we watch out for, especially around the kids, but people surprise you."

I watch Wanda and the doctor shake hands. Wanda walks away. She does not look back.

If you think about it, it's very, very clever. The drugs in my system. An alleged fall down the stairs to explain the bruising around my eye, which I'm just now starting to feel. And since they've clearly decided I'm not an undercover cop, who cares what happens to me as long as I leave?

I look at my backpack, lying there innocently on a chair. I think about Wanda going through it while I was in the kitchen, pawing my meager possessions, taking note of my ID, copying my personal information down, sniffing my toiletries and judging the condition of my underwear. I decide then and there that they couldn't possibly think I'm a cop. To them, I'm an unknown. They couldn't find anything in the backpack, but they seem to know I'm not with the law. Which means that I'm utterly expendable. At first, they were interested in finding out what I want. Now, that's no longer the case. They just want me gone.

The almost crippling nausea ebbs but doesn't go away for a long time. After a few tests, the doctor decides against pumping my stomach, and settles for giving me an antinauseant and hooking me up to an IV. The nurse asks me if she can call a cab to the ferry that will take me back to Vancouver.

"Sure," I say. I turn my phone on, but there are no messages. Seb and Leo must be too busy enjoying their staycation to check in. That's okay. I'll talk to them soon enough.

When I get to the ferry terminal, I watch the cab turn around after picking up a passenger from the ferry that just came in. I buy an assortment of snacks from the vending machine and a ginger ale to wash it all down. Then I wait until the ferry departs. It only takes a moment of silence with the night, the ocean, the trees behind me, to recalibrate. I'm no longer hallucinating, so I can appreciate the beauty in front of me. This island is so stunning it almost hurts. What a perfect place to set up a sex cult that is clearly so much more than a sex cult.

It's not even 9 A.M. but the sun is shining brightly. I sling my backpack over my shoulder and head back into town. A helpful employee of BC Ferries allows me to hitch a ride, and seems happy to share some salt and vinegar chips with me along the way.

"What's the deal with Spring Love Farm?" I ask. "I'm thinking of volunteering with them."

"Oh, you should! They're a staple at the farmers' market, and they send their produce all over the lower mainland. Their stall at the market used to have blackberry-apple pies that were to die for."

"But not anymore?"

"No," she says, frowning. "Not anymore. I wonder why."

I don't. Baking is a fine art. They must be too busy

poisoning people to put in the time. By my count, they have already poisoned me twice. Once with the cocoa last night, whatever they'd put in there masked by the bitter dark drink that someone handed to me. I didn't finish it, but I remember the nausea and lightheadedness started within an hour of my first sip. The odd look on Cheyenne's face when I poured the rest of the drink in the fire. The second time was with the green smoothie, and it hit me like a train because I was so out of it and thirsty that I drank the whole thing.

Despite Wanda's act back at the hospital, she couldn't hide her true intentions. The people at Spring Love wanted me to leave by any means necessary. They made me sick to get me off the property because they thought it would keep me away.

They were wrong.

Chapter 6

AFTER PURCHASING TWO liters of water in plastic jugs, I take a room in a cheap inn, which seems the safest bet to stay out of sight for now.

The painkillers are a temptation that I give into because my shoulder hurts too much to let me sleep easily. I pop two of them and wash them down with a glass of water. The greater temptation is to reach for something stronger than water, but I have kicked that particular habit with great difficulty. When Bonnie went missing, I started drinking again, after many hard difficult years of sobriety. It was stupid, and I've regretted it ever since, especially since it took every ounce of my willpower to stop. Whisper had been unhappy with my regression—I could feel it. So whenever I want a drink, I imagine the judgment in my dog's eyes, which is what I do now.

The toilets in this inn smell faintly of sulphur, which

is normal on the islands. That's okay. Unpleasant, but not much of a bother. The bed isn't comfortable, but I sleep anyway. I wake after an hour, drink some more water and eat a power bar, the remainder of my vending-machine snacks. The cramps are gone, and now there's only a lingering headache. By the time I call Leo, I'm feeling much, much better than I did this morning. I am refreshed and unpoisoned, and there isn't a whole lot in life better than that.

"Okay, wait. They *poisoned* you?" Leo asks, after I explained to him the events of the past twenty-four hours. "With *psychedelic mushrooms*?"

"I won't be able to prove it. It's their word against mine."

Leo is appalled. "Nora, get on the next ferry back! I'll take over from here."

"No. What about your staycation?"

"Come on. It will be fine to leave this one to me after all you've been through. Besides, Seb has a few meetings today, so I guess the staycation of our dreams is over." There's a little hitch in his voice. "Who even came up with the idea of a staycation anyway? It's ridiculous. I don't know what I was thinking. Look, I know you probably want to do this on your own, and we can't really afford to have more than one person on this case, but to hell with it. I could use the distraction. And I'm supposed to be supervising you a little more closely anyway."

If it were just about the supervision, I would protest. But it's not. Leo's sadness over his disappointing staycation is too great to ignore. I would rather do this on my own, but I could use his help. "Come over. I'll meet you in town and we'll work on it together."

"You're not leaving before you figure this out, are you?"

"No."

"Well, I should have expected that. I can catch the next ferry. I should be there by evening."

"We need more on Vikram Sharma. He's the key." I can't forget his voice, telling those workers to get back to bed.

"On it," Leo says. "See you soon."

"Wait, how's Whisper?"

"Seb took her with him today, so she's doing just fine."

"To his meetings?"

"Yeah. Apparently I'm a distraction, but she's not." He hangs up.

I don't blame Seb for choosing Whisper as his companion for the day. I would do the same thing, but I'm not in a committed relationship with one of the nicest men on the planet. Leo's sadness and disappointment bothers me, but it's none of my business. It's just not like Seb to be this inconsiderate. I have been in their lives since they fell in love and I'm getting the feeling that I'm watching them fall out of it. Now I'm disappointed and sad, too. But I can't let that distract me. Ken Barnes agreed to our quote, which included a budget for expenses. The budget is fair, but not exactly generous. We don't have that much time to bring him information on his son's welfare, and we really haven't made much progress.

A ten-minute walk takes me to the center of the Ganges village, by the harbor. It's small, quaint. In the mid-morning light, it looks like the most innocent place in the world. Blue skies and blue ocean. Pretty boats on the water. I even see some paddle boarders out, a few doing yoga on their boards, as if this hippy shit can't be contained on land and must spread out onto the ocean, too.

One of the yoga paddle boarders loses balance and topples into the water. I choke back a surprised laugh because karma is not only a bitch, but she also has a great sense of humor, and that's when the teenage girl from last night comes up to me and shoves at my shoulders. Not enough to send me flying, but enough to set me off balance.

"Leave us alone!" she says, her eyes ablaze with a righteous fury that I don't understand. "We need this job!"

I'm too shocked to do anything but stare as she turns on her heel, yanks the strap of her heavy backpack, which had slipped down her arm, and stalks away. It takes me a moment to go after her, and since she had the element of surprise I lose her in the grocery store, a large chain.

What was that about?

It reminds me of something Cheyenne said. About Salt Spring historically being a refuge for the black community. Maybe it's still perceived as some kind of refuge. In the past year there has been a spike of asylum seekers crossing into Vancouver from the Peace Arch park in Washington. They are mostly people of color, like this teenager. If Spring Love is using migrant labor, maybe this is a way for the undocumented to make some money while their claims are being processed. And maybe it would appeal to someone's romantic notions of revisiting history. But then why isolate them at the farm and have them come to the kitchens at different times? Why the separation?

Maybe there's something they don't want these workers to see.

I leave the grocery-store parking lot. Ganges is surprisingly busy, which makes me wonder if there's something going on. Sure enough, I see stalls set up for the Saturday farmers' market. On the chance that my system is able to handle something more substantial than a vending-machine snack, I get a small coffee and a breakfast sandwich from a nearby cafe. Then I sit outside to watch the market.

Though the market is in full swing, the Spring Love stall is bare. Within a few minutes, however, the farm's pickup truck pulls up and I watch Vikram, Cheyenne, and Trevor unload the produce from the back. Their stall is smaller than the others, with less available for purchase. They do brisk business, but that is owed largely to Vikram and Cheyenne's personal touch. They give warm smiles and handshakes to everyone who shows interest. Trevor is a nice addition to the picture—a thin, silent boy who doesn't smile but works the cash box, taking money, counting change, and putting purchases in paper bags for the customers.

An efficient operation, sure, but there's something that bothers me about it. It's like the act of a play performed for an audience that's content to accept what is shown without even attempting to scratch off the surface veneer. As I continue to take them in, I realize it's an insult, a farce. Vikram and Cheyenne are no more interested in selling farm-fresh produce than I am. It's only Trevor who seems to notice this. He watches them carefully from behind the cash. It's not obvious, but my years in foster care have taught me a little bit about reading a child's body language. He looks to Cheyenne for instructions, but ignores Vikram completely. Pretending, I think, that Vikram doesn't exist. It's subtle and invisible to everyone around him, but I am certain that Trevor hates his mother's new boyfriend.

I buy another cup of coffee. After another hour or so, the market dies down. People begin to pack up. Trevor whispers something to Cheyenne. She issues him some kind of warning. He nods and walks toward the harbor, within her line of sight.

It takes me a few minutes to reach his side. I'm careful to circle around the market so I'm not seen, but I experience a moment of hesitation anyway. Then I put it out of my mind. Cheyenne and Vikram will realize I'm here sooner or later. I'm not about to hide.

I find Trevor watching the boats out on the water. "Did you get a chance to practice the guitar today?" I ask.

He looks at me. "I'm not supposed to talk to you. Vik says it was bad to learn the guitar from you and you can't be trusted."

"Did it upset you when he put his hand on your shoulder last night at the fire pit?" Because it sure as hell bothered me.

And just like that, a mask slips onto his face.

He says nothing, so I continue, in a lighter tone this time. "I don't think your mom and dad like me very much."

"Vik isn't my dad," he informs me. "And they don't like you because they think you're a liar."

"Do you think I'm a liar?"

He shrugs. "I heard them say they thought you might have been a cop, but then after, they said you weren't. I could have told them that you weren't."

"Oh yeah? What makes you think I'm not a cop?" I ask, amused.

"You just don't look like one. My real dad is a lawyer and he knows all about stuff like that."

"Would you live with him if you could?"

Another shrug. It is clear neither of us are great at conversation, but at least I'm trying. "You know what

I was wondering about? When I came to Spring Love, there was a building, right off the path to the fields that looked kind of like a barn? What's it for?"

"That's where the farm workers stay. I'm not really allowed to go there or talk to them, though."

"Why?"

"Because Vikram says their English isn't good."

I pause. "Isn't that why you *should* talk to them? So it can get better?"

"I guess so, but *he* doesn't even talk to them. They just work in the fields away from everybody. He gets them to load the truck and he does the selling at the market. He mostly works up where the people come to do yoga, with my mom. Hey," he says, an idea striking him suddenly, "you gonna come back and help me learn the guitar?"

"Are you going to come back?" says Cheyenne, from behind us. Trevor stiffens. She doesn't sound angry, but both Trevor and I know without a doubt that she is. "Go on, say it again."

Trevor looks at me but doesn't back down. My respect for him grows immensely. "Are you going to come back and help me learn the guitar?"

"I don't know, buddy." There's a small urge to pat his shoulder, but I know it wouldn't be welcome. He's looking from me to his mother with watchful eyes.

"Say goodbye to Nora, sweetheart," Cheyenne says. "I don't think she'll be joining us again."

"Bye, Nora."

"Bye, Trevor. If you want to get better at the guitar, make sure you practice."

He nods solemnly at this. If I never see him again, at least I've given him some of the work ethic I've lost along the way. "I will," he says, then he leaves with his mother, who is busy whispering into his ear. About the importance of choosing one's friends carefully, I imagine.

I watch them go, feeling a clash of emotions. Poisoning aside, this is becoming more than just a job. Trevor obviously has two parents that care very much for him. Ken wants to protect him from Cheyenne, and Cheyenne wants to protect him from the riffraff of the world, like myself. As well as the decent laborers, who he is also not allowed to talk to. If she wants to keep him stuck on an island with no music to soothe his soul, that's not the worst thing I can imagine, by a long shot. But to keep him separated from the farm's workers tells me my suspicions are warranted.

I don't surround myself with children and I was never part of my own daughter's upbringing, but I understand that this child is somehow different. Far too old for his age. You get kids like this in foster care, where I was brought up. Hell, I was one of them myself. But I've never seen it in someone like Trevor, whose mother has taken him from the city and thrust him into a place like this, where nature reigns. He should be a happy child, but he's not. It's like he's seen things far beyond his years and they have marked him, made him retreat into himself.

I had decided to continue with this case because someone fucked with my digestive system and it made me mad. Now I'm staying on because something about this kid reminds me of myself when I was a child, something behind his eyes telling me that he's keeping secrets he shouldn't even have been exposed to. I'm going to find out what they are, and I'm going to do it for him.

Chapter 7

THERE ARE STILL a few stalls up when I get to the market grounds. Lucky for me, Alive Farms does not care one bit that the market is over and they should pack up and leave. They have vegetables and baked goods to offer and no one is going to stop the tall brunette manning the stall from staying here until she dies or sells out.

I don't have to fake interest in the last blackberry-apple pie on display. My mouth salivates at the sight of it. "Ten dollars," she says. "I'll give you a special price because it's the last one." She looks too fine boned to be a farmhand of any kind, but when she rolls up her sleeves I see the strength of her forearms.

"Is it as good as the pies Spring Love used to sell?"

Her voice goes cold. "It's better. I bake them myself."

"You're their neighbor, aren't you?"

"That's right. We border them." She isn't interested in selling me a discounted pie any longer, as I've managed not only to insult her but also to be nosy at the same time. Well, you can't please everybody.

From my web research, Alive seems to be a cheerful little operation compared to Spring Love. Their property is only a third of the size, but they are consistently rated highly for the quality of their produce, which makes sense. There are no yoga retreats at Alive to distract them. Nor do they seem to care much about "harmonious living." They are a farm, and by all online accounts, a very good one.

"I'll take the pie," I say, pulling out my wallet and handing her a twenty. This defrosts her ever so slightly, but it's enough to give me an in. As she makes change, I add, "I'm thinking about their yoga retreat. Have you done one?"

She snorts. "Ha, like I would ever. Good luck with that. You don't seem the type."

"What does that mean?"

"You're not wearing designer clothes and you seem to have all your marbles, that's what. Not sure you'll fit in."

"I don't really fit in anywhere." Which is the truth.

"Well, it sure as heck ain't going to be there. Damn shame, if you ask me. Spring Love used to be a big part of this island's community, but they barely show up to our events anymore. Everything's about those retreats. Fancy people get on the ferry, drive out in their Mercedes that can't take the roads and a couple days later they drive back. Nobody comes into town and buys anything."

"You never see the yoga students at the market?"

"Never. Vikram and Cheyenne don't even show up when they've got one of those things on. They send Wanda. She used to bake the pies, actually. It was her family that owned the property before Vikram. The Washingtons had some history here, but Wanda was an only child and," she lowers her voice, "turns out she can't have kids. She and Vikram were sweethearts of a kind, once. Then he left and, I hear, got into some trouble with the law. When he moved back, he bought the farm from her and it was never the same again. Took up with Cheyenne even though Wanda was still living on the grounds. Shame, but I don't blame him. Cheyenne's a better-looking version of Wanda."

I don't let on how mean-spirited I find this. I smile in what I hope is a conspiratorial manner. "I met him once. I don't think we got along very well."

"Oh, you didn't get along with the fake doctor who ain't really a doctor anymore?" she asks. But this is maybe a step too far. When she realizes what she's said, she blushes, then becomes angry. "I'd stay away from that place if I were you."

She turns away and begins packing up the stall. I try

a few times to make eye contact, but she won't look at me anymore.

The thing I hate about small towns, villages, islands, and general inbred enclaves of the world is that everybody is all up in everyone else's business. Constantly. There can be no secrets here, only things kept from outsiders until someone loosens up over something as trivial as pie. The thing I love about these places is that it only takes one disgruntled member of the community to reveal the totality of someone's personal history.

So Vikram got a piece of property that he might have wanted and traded up—which leaves Wanda to pick up the pieces and run the farm.

What's in it for her?

And what did the Alive Farms woman mean by "fake doctor who ain't really a doctor anymore"?

AT THE ISLAND'S archives on the second floor of the public library, I go through old newspapers on island life. It seems idyllic enough, low crime rates. No place, however, is as innocent as it seems, because people love to keep secrets. Trevor, for example, and the truth about his feelings toward Vikram.

A black-and-white picture from 1929 catches my attention. It's of a group of schoolchildren gathered for a photo. The diversity I see staring back at me is astonishing. Black, white, and indigenous children are at school together, side by side. I've never seen anything like it. People keep saying there's black history on this island, but I don't see much of that on the faces of Salt Spring's current residents—Cheyenne and Wanda being the exceptions. In this photo, I see evidence that there had been a black community here, and that this particular island school was integrated. The last segregated school in Canada closed in 1983, whereas the United States banned school segregation in the 1950s. The last residential school in Canada closed in 1996. The racism in Canada's education systems is hardly ever discussed, but it has always been there.

In this photo, however, you could imagine a better future. In 1929, these kids were learning together.

And I understand Cheyenne better than ever.

I'd given my birth daughter away for adoption when she was born, and put her from my mind. I could not allow myself to think of her because becoming a mother wasn't a choice I'd made for myself. My loving her the way she deserved was out of the question. But if I had chosen motherhood, and I'd had some freedom of movement, I might have brought her here. To live out her childhood in a place where, even in the 1920s, children could stand next to each other and not feel that any of their peers were "less than."

I don't know if this island was as much of a utopia as it seems in this photo—it couldn't possibly have been that idyllic—but I might have wanted to come and see, just for her. Her cultural identity is even more confusing than my own, though that in and of itself is a hard thought to grasp. Bonnie's father was Chinese. I am part indigenous and part something else I've never discovered. I would like her to live somewhere all this doesn't matter. Where she can be accepted regardless of the color of her skin. In an ideal world, it would be different for her than it was for me. We're not in an ideal world, but a woman can have dreams.

For some reason, this picture hurts, just a little too much.

It's almost a relief to move past, and to continue through the archives. School photos and photos of children are of particular interest to me. I ate half a pie before coming to the library, but my thirst has been insatiable since this morning. Even though my throat is parched, I refuse to leave until I've gotten what I came for.

It's only when my discomfort is almost unbearable that I find it.

The cast photo from a school play shows a Romeo onstage and a Juliet up on a makeshift balcony. The Juliet is miscast. She doesn't seem the type to laze about on balconies, waiting for boys to come rescue her. She's the kind of girl who will go out and get the boy and persuade him that even though he's divorced her, he should still buy her family's farm and let her stay on it. Even though he wants to move on, he really shouldn't, because she's decided to have him in her life, no matter what.

Young Wanda gazes at Young Vikram with a look so possessive that I can feel it through the years, through the distance of a photograph. I can feel the love. And it isn't just one-sided, either, at least not back then.

And by Vikram, I mean Vincent, which is his real first name, according to the description beneath the photograph. Wanda Washington and Vincent Sharma were once very much in love.

Chapter 8

LEO COMES TO town looking jaunty. There is no other word for it. He gets out of his car wearing a crisp, patterned shirt, open at the neck, navy shorts, chocolate brown loafers and gold-rimmed aviator shades. He swings a distressed cocoa weekender bag from hand to hand and smiles at me like we are long lost lovers, meeting at last for an island rendezvous. I resist the urge to look behind me to check if all this effort is being made for someone with much better personal style than myself.

Leo is trying so very hard to be happy. Seeing him now, I'm glad he's decided to come. I meet him in my summer cargo pants and a faded gray T-shirt, looking like his homeless sidekick or possibly his drug dealer.

I hand over what's left of the pie and we get straight to business. After I fill him in on what I discovered in the archives, he frowns. "Vincent Sharma? That name sounds vaguely familiar, but I'm not sure why."

"Could it have something to do with what the woman from Alive Farms said? She told me he was a fake doctor that's not really a doctor anymore. So maybe he'd been a doctor once."

"And now he's just a fake?"

I'm confused, too. "On the Spring Love website there's nothing about Vincent's—or Vikram's—accreditation in anything other than yoga."

"He does look like a yogi," says Leo, pulling up Vincent's photo from the website. I know a little too much about him to see it with fresh eyes, but when I first looked at it my initial impression of him was of someone serene. The thin frame, long hair and East Indian features give him the appearance of an ascetic. In my imagination, I can see him on a mountaintop, sitting cross-legged with his hands on his knees and a breeze blowing through his dark locks. There are people who would pay good money for that kind of serenity. Not me, of course, but other people, ones with better incomes. Who enjoy sitting on the ground, maybe.

Now, looking at him, I can't ignore that there's something staged about this picture. It's too glossy, too perfect. It feels like branding. Yes, that's it. I'm starting to think that Vikram-Vincent Sharma isn't really a yoga instructor at all. Which leaves me wondering what they're doing up at that retreat.

"Did you pack any workout gear?" I ask Leo.

"Are you thinking of yoga pants?"

"Very, very tight yoga pants."

He grins. "We're in luck. I brought the tightest possible yoga pants a grown man is legally allowed to wear."

"The innocent people at Spring Love are in for a serious treat."

"I sense sarcasm, Nora, and I just want you to know that it's uncalled for. I take leg day very seriously and these stems aren't meant to be hidden away."

Now that he's mentioned it, I realize he has been working out a lot more than usual lately and his legs really do look fantastic. He looks like so many of the other fit men in and around Vancouver. Unhappy, but with great stems.

As it turns out, the tightest possible yoga pants a grown man is legally allowed to wear aren't all that tight. They're made of stretchy material, though, and tapered at the bottom where they hit just below the knee. "So that you don't accidentally flash the goods during hot yoga," Leo explains. "I mean, at those kinds of classes you're almost delirious, so it's not like it would matter too much if there was slippage, but still. Some things I like to save for the bedroom."

Hmm. Good to know.

We're in my room at the inn. They are all booked up for the night, so it looks like we're sharing. "Any luck getting through to the retreat?" I ask, to steer the conversation away from "slippage," which is a mental image I do not want to have.

"No one's answering the number they have online. I sent an email inquiring about the next session, but nothing there, either. Are you sure they said they were having something that starts tomorrow?"

"Yes." Cheyenne was pretty clear about that.

"Hell, if they don't want to take my money . . ."

"You mean Ken Barnes's money?"

"Of course. On my way over here, I told him that there's been a development in the case and we'll have to stay on a few days extra."

"Did you tell him I was poisoned?"

"No, but I did tell him you got ill from something in the food. He sounded excited that it might show the environment may not be good for children . . . Nora, what do you think is going on over there? I mean, it's a farm that's not really a farm. A yoga retreat that may not really be a yoga retreat. I don't think you're imagining things. If you say they poisoned you, they poisoned you. They tell the world they're open and welcoming, but they don't actually want outsiders there. What are they hiding?"

Trust doesn't come easily to me, never has. Growing up in the system, you learn from an early age that trust is a delicate thing. It's a give and take. It's more intimate than love because it's based on respect. You can love someone you don't respect, but trust and respect go hand in hand. You can't have one without the other. I have never told Leo how important it is that he trusts me, even to the extent that I've told him a truly outrageous story of being poisoned at a racially harmonious commune and he simply believes me without question or challenge. That's something money can't buy.

Some part of me wants to share all this with him, to tell him how much it means to me, but the reason he's here on Salt Spring is because he's battling with his emotions. I can't talk to him about trust because it might make him think of the man in his life he's starting to lose trust in. It's probably for the best. I'm not great at talking about this, anyway. It's enough, for me, that I feel it. I hope he feels it, too.

"I'm not sure what's going on," I say.

"But you're worried, I can tell. Is it about Trevor?"

"I don't know. He doesn't like Vikram but I don't know why."

"It could be that he resents Vikram for replacing his father."

"Could be."

"That's a tough position for any kid to be in. My parents got divorced when I was around the same age and I resented them both for it for a long time. Hard feelings for the new man in a boy's life is normal . . . unless you think there's more of a reason to be worried. Catch any signs of abuse?"

I shake my head. Nothing I've seen can be considered abuse but, then again, I haven't seen all that much.

Yet. "I'd love to talk to those people who actually work the farm. They've been isolated, but that doesn't mean they're stupid. Someone might have seen something."

"So that's the plan, then? I show up for the yoga retreat, see what I can find, and you try to get to the farm workers?"

"We'll see if they'll talk to me."

"The girl you saw earlier said something about needing the job, so they might be closemouthed to keep their employment. If they're undocumented or being processed for refugee claims, the only thing they're more scared of than losing work is getting deported. It could be a pressure point." He hesitates. "I'm not comfortable scaring people who just want to work."

Neither am I. I've been desperate for work, too. "I won't threaten them." I might not have to. People often draw their own conclusions. But there's no use borrowing trouble tonight.

"Okay, all we're really looking for is something that shows this is an unsuitable environment for a child." He pauses, scratches the stubble on his chin.

"What is it?"

"The name Vincent Sharma. I've heard it before and it's been bothering me since you mentioned it. How about you try to get some sleep and I'll do some digging?"

"You're not tired?"

"Not even a little bit."

I'm usually the night owl in the operation, but I'm not fully recovered from yesterday so I don't protest too much. I pull the covers over my head and fall into a deep, untroubled sleep, while Leo taps away at his laptop.

When I wake, it's morning.

Leo is curled up on the carpeted floor with a pillow tucked under his head, snoring lightly. The window is cracked open and I can smell the sea, even from here. It's a pull I can't resist. A walk down to the harbor calms the now familiar nausea I'm once again feeling. The ocean gives me no answers today, but the view almost makes it worth the ferry ride I took to get over here. Almost. Maybe existing on pie at my age isn't such a great idea, but I don't regret it. It was excellent pie, well worth the ten dollars I'd paid for it. The information I'd gotten from the woman at the stall was worth it, too.

Despite its reputation Spring Love Farm doesn't seem to be all that popular here on the island.

I bring coffee and breakfast sandwiches back to the room. Leo is already awake and dressed. "Where are we at with Vikram Sharma?" I ask.

"Nowhere. Found one woman named Elizabeth Rathburn, who wrote about seeing the light at a Spring Love retreat and swears by his therapy. Besides that, I can't find a thing on him. No social media, no news articles. Nothing under Vincent or Vikram. I emailed Sebastian to see if he remembers anything."

"What did he say?"

"No response yet." Leo looks away. I don't bring up the fact that Seb is usually always connected to his phone, because Leo already knows that. That Seb hasn't responded during the night he has spent away from his partner . . . it doesn't look good.

But Leo clearly doesn't want to talk about it, thank God. "Okay," he says. "It's best we're not seen at Spring Love together, so how about I go first and you follow this afternoon?"

"Sure. They might make you hand over your phone, so be prepared."

"Here, you better take this." He hands me a compact digital camera with a powerful zoom lens. For most of our work there's not much we don't do on our phones, but if we need better-quality photos, we bring out better equipment. Especially for infidelity cases. People like to see the close-ups on those. Infidelity and sometimes child custody—when it comes to loved ones, they want to see the goods.

Before he leaves, he gives me a sad sort of smile. "If they don't let me into the retreat, I'll hang around and see what I can find."

"Good luck today."

"You too, Nora." He pauses at the door. "You know, it's crazy that you're only now working on your license. You've been good for the company. I'm glad to have you around . . . okay, I'm done making you uncomfortable now. Let's get this job over with," he says, grinning suddenly.

It's nice of Leo to say all that but I have a bad feeling about this plan, and about Spring Love in general. I keep quiet, though, because the last thing we need right now is to give in to doubts.

Leo's right, the sooner we get this job done, the better. For everyone involved, but especially for Trevor Barnes, the ten-year-old boy with so much sadness in his eyes it is almost unbearable.

Chapter 9

I DON'T HEAR from Leo by noon, so I head away from town on foot. Before packing up, I'd noticed he'd left his phone charger plugged into the wall, so I made sure to put it in my backpack, which I stash at the inn's luggage storage.

It doesn't take much walking for the sweat to cover me completely and dust from the road to settle in the creases of my eyelids and tangle with my eyelashes. The afternoon sun is high in the sky by the time I finally manage to hitch a ride to Alive Farms and walk toward Spring Love. About midway between the two farms, I duck through a gap in the fence and approach Spring Love through the woods. The forest immediately closes in on me. The shadows from the trees cast long, reaching fingers, sending welcome frissons of coolness over my heated limbs.

In the shade of the trees, and growing in the damp moss underneath fallen logs, I see clusters of mushrooms growing. Seemingly innocent. Magic mushrooms, I have learned, are only magical because of the psilocybin they contain. A potent psychedelic. In addition to the mushrooms, I also spot some poison oak scattered through these woods, as well.

In just a few hours this morning, I have attempted to become something of an Internet expert on the classification of poisonous plants, with limited success. I'm pretty sure about the oak, but I'm just guessing about the mushrooms. I make sure to take photos, but as the shadows deepen I head toward the main compound with greater urgency, thinking how easy it had been for them to poison me if these woods were their source. I wonder if someone had walked into this forest as soon as Vikram had spotted me to collect a sample of a toxic plant. Poison, they say, is a woman's weapon, but I personally blame Vikram for no reason other than his lies.

I watch the compound. Dusk falls late here this time of year, so there's still some light out. Cheyenne, Vikram, and Wanda are noticeably absent, but I do see Kelly, the cook, moving from the schoolhouse to the kitchens.

Taking a chance that the workers are still in the fields and the others are up at the yoga retreat, I slip around to the side entrance of the main building, careful to keep away from the kitchens. Again, I'm struck by how empty this place is, that for a commune it isn't very communal.

During the initial tour, Vikram explained this building was separated into the sleeping areas for men and women who didn't live in one of the yurts, with the huge dining room being the main focus, and the kitchens toward the back.

But there was a door he'd passed straight by, which is what I head toward now. The door is locked, but it's nothing I can't get through. It takes me under a minute with the slim lock-pick kit from my back pocket. I put the picks back and enter the room quietly. It's an office, simply furnished. The framed certificates on the wall announce that Wanda Washington is, in reality, Dr. Wanda Washington, and that she is a registered psychologist.

Well, hell. I know the job market is tough, but psychology to farm management is a bit of a stretch. There are no appointments in the leather-bound book by the phone, but the desk is full of paperwork pertaining to running Spring Love. Wanda seems to be in charge of it all, her handwriting on everything from invoices to deposit slips. I go back and look carefully through the leather book. There are no appointments, true, but every month, three days are blocked off. This month, the three-day block starts today. So, once a month they have a yoga retreat—but it's not marked as such, and they don't answer phone calls about it, either.

The phone rings, as though I summoned it. The ring startles me into answering, if only to make it shut up. "Hello?"

"Hi, is this Spring Love?"

"Yes, can I help you?"

"Yes, my brother Gary went over to your yoga retreat today. Can I speak to him?"

"No, I'm afraid that's not possible."

"Please, it's important. He left his medication at home and I need to know if he needs me to bring them for him."

"What medication?"

"It's for his depression. He'll know which ones I'm talking about. But he also left behind his multivitamin, too, so I guess I could also bring those?"

"Okay, I'll pass along the message."

"Is there a way you can get him on the phone? I was able to check in with him the last time he was there."

"No, we don't disturb participants of the retreat while they're . . . in session. But I'll make sure he gets the message."

She's not happy about this. "What's your name?"

"Wanda Washington," I say, before placing the receiver back on its cradle.

By the time I make it outside, I'm more confused than ever about Vikram-Vincent and Wanda. Nobody here seems to be who they say they are.

Through the dining-room windows I see the community's kids gathered with Kelly and the school-teacher, Shoshanna. Trevor is sitting at the far end of the table. He's not alone, but he might as well be. There's something about the solitude in this kid that eats away at me. A few clicks of the camera later, and I'm on my way down the path to the barn. Based on my first and last night at Spring Love, I know the workers will wait until the others have cleared out to access the kitchen.

Nobody pops out to stop me, even though I keep expecting it. This is a working farm. The path down to it shouldn't be this silent. When I get to the converted barn, I see why. There is no one here. The same side window I'd peeked through a couple nights ago is still cracked a bit. I open it further and hoist myself into the bathroom, feeling the very lack of human presence as soon as I enter. A cursory search tells me the building has been separated into two sleeping quarters with about six cots in each and another bathroom at the opposite end of the building. There's little privacy to be found in these living quarters, but maybe the people who stay here aren't meant to stay long enough for it to matter.

It's possible they're supposed to be a source of transient labor but the speed with which these people have packed up is impressive. Maybe they'd been forced out sooner than they'd expected, which would explain why the girl who shoved me had that heavy backpack with her. And she'd clearly believed that it was somehow my fault.

From the emptiness of this barn, from its lack of soul and air of abandon, I see these workers are only meant to support the illusion of a farm. Just like the bare minimum Vikram and Cheyenne had done at the farmers' market. An illusion. A charade. But why?

There are no answers here.

I leave the same way I came in, careful to crack the window just the way I found it. When I turn, a small, thin figure is waiting for me. We consider each other in the deepening shadows of dusk, Trevor and I, until he relaxes his shoulders and moves a few steps closer.

"What are you doing out here?" I ask softly.

"I saw you watching me from the dining room."

"Well, you better get back before someone misses you."

"No one will. Everyone thinks I'm watching movies with Frank and his dad. We usually watch at least two."

"And Frank and his dad don't know you're supposed to be watching movies with them, huh? Where's your mom and Vikram?" I ask.

A sly look comes over his face. "I'll show you if you teach me to play the guitar."

I think seriously about leaving right now with Trevor, delivering him to Ken and letting him sort it all out with Trevor in a safer place. But I have no proof that something wrong is happening here, nothing but a feeling, a glimpse at a boy's face when he looks at his mother's new man. No matter how much I want to take Trevor away, I need to show Ken Barnes something other than shadowy photos of an empty barn.

This might be my one shot at getting it.

"Deal," I say, holding out my hand. He shakes it solemnly, his small hand bony and strong in mine.

"We gotta go this way," he says, heading to the woods.

Trevor leads me using a path that only he can see. When I go back to Vancouver, Leo and I will hand over photos that may imply these woods are dangerous for children to be in unsupervised, but that won't be the truth. Trevor knows this place, where to place his feet exactly to avoid making noise. How to walk sure in a forest. How to be quick. I lose all sense of direction as darkness falls around us, but I feel no fear, just a building curiosity.

"Who's your favorite guitar player?" he asks.

"Sister Rosetta Tharpe."

"A girl?"

"You got a problem with that?" I ask. He shakes his head solemnly. "Who's yours?"

"I don't have one yet."

"That's okay. You been practicing?"

"Not so much, but I will."

I smile at the promise in his voice.

We keep walking. It hasn't been that long, I think, but the dusk somehow feels endless. It's darker here in the woods, but I can still see. I sense light, winking at me through the tree cover. Several short, halting steps take me out of the woods, and in the clearing is a two-story lodge, shining brightly at us, the exterior of it lit up by LED bulbs. There are lights on inside, but no movement can be discerned beyond the heavy vertical blinds. Four luxury cars and the Spring Love pickup are parked on the gravel road leading to the building. I'm getting my bearings again. This isn't the main road to the compound, so it must be a private entrance—one that is noticeably absent from the drawn map of the property on the Spring Love website.

It's getting darker by the minute. There is, however, enough light on the cars to take several quick photos of the license plates. Leo, who I haven't heard from all day, might have already gotten this information, but it can't hurt to be thorough. When I turn back to Trevor, I find him looking from me to the camera. "What's that for?" he asks.

"It's for work. Hey, how do you get in this place?"

He takes me around back and shows me the private staircase leading to an apartment suite. The key is under a rock, which I would have found in seconds even if he hadn't shown it to me. "Mom says to only use this if there's an emergency." Which means she wanted him to always have easy access to her.

"But you come here all the time." I see it in his expression, by the way he looks down and scuffs his shoes into the dirt. "Don't worry, I won't tell. I'm going to go inside to see your mom. Do you want to come with me?"

A strange look comes over his face. He shakes his head.

"Okay, I'm going to go in for a few minutes, but I want you to wait for me. Will you do that?"

He nods.

"Don't leave without saying goodbye," I say.

"What's your number?" he asks, pulling out a cell phone.

I laugh. "Where did you get that?"

"My dad gave it to me. He said to keep it a secret."

"What's the number?"

"I don't know, only my dad calls me on it."

"You can have mine." I put my number into his phone and call it so his number is recorded on mine, as well. "Here, just in case something happens out here and you need to talk to me. I'll be right back, okay?"

"Okay."

I wait for several minutes after he leaves, wanting to make sure he's far enough away before I open the door. Whatever is in there, I know it's the source of that odd look that came across his face. Trevor knows where his mom goes when she disappears for the three days Wanda has marked off on her calendar because he has made it his business to find out. But he clearly doesn't want to see it again.

I'm about to find out why.

Chapter 10

I WALK THROUGH a small, chaotic apartment full of scarves, healing crystals, and rock lamps glowing amber. It smells of incense, but the scent is mild enough that it doesn't really bother me. The hardwood floor is clean and beautifully varnished, with meditation pillows scattered through the room. It's clear this is someone's private sanctuary. Someone annoying, obviously. The kind of person who sits on the floor—not out of poverty, but in an attempt to be one with their surroundings. A person who meditates and lights incense. I have a feeling this room is Vikram's but there's nothing overtly masculine or feminine about it. How very Zen.

Next to the en suite bathroom is a door that was meant to be locked but isn't. The door has been left slightly ajar, as though the last person in here left in haste. The lock is the same on Wanda's office, but I'm glad I don't need to waste time with my lock-pick kit. I have the camera ready when I enter the cool, dark room.

Flicking on the lights, I stop and stare.

There is a long steel table containing lab equipment I can't identify and several large plastic containers, lids off, where a small variety of mushrooms grow. A freezer in the corner of the room is filled with more of the same, but frozen.

I have a strong feeling these aren't the kind of mushrooms you simply toss into your pasta.

I'm not sure what I expected, but a small-scale grow op isn't it. I see now why it was so easy for them to slip me some hallucinogenic action, at the quantity that would be toxic enough to make me sick. Not very child friendly, is it?

It does, however, make for exciting photographic opportunities.

The memory card on the camera is full, so I make sure to take enough photos with my phone, too. Just in case. I'm about to leave the room when a call comes in from Seb. "Nora, I've been trying to get in touch with Leo," he says, when I answer.

"He went to a yoga retreat. He either doesn't have his phone with him or the battery died." I don't think Leo has gone without charging his phone for more than a few hours a day.

"What? Why is he at a yoga retreat?"

I sketch out the details of the case, while I turn off

the lights and leave the room. "Leo hasn't been able to find much on Vincent Sharma, but he knows he's heard the name before."

"He has," Seb says. "You familiar with Hollywood House? It was a private hospital in Vancouver where, during the sixties, people with money could pay to be treated with psychedelic drugs. They'd get assessments, counseling, the works. There was a lesser-known facility in Victoria called the Wash Clinic that did the same thing, but when the Manson murders happened, that kind of research was shut down and the doctors that were interested in it were pushed to the fringes. The doctor spearheading the Wash Clinic research moved to Salt Spring Island in the late eighties to take over some property he inherited after the clinic had gone bust. His name was Clyde Washington. I interviewed him for a story on LSD a while back. I think it had something to do with Cary Grant."

"The actor?"

"Folks were big into psychedelics back then and Hollywood was more open to it than most. But Nora, the reason I called is Leo sent a message last night asking me if I recognized the name Vincent Sharma. I only got the message this morning, but yes, yes I do know Vincent. I spoke to him once."

"For what?"

"That interview with Washington. I'm looking through my notes right now. At the time, Vincent Sharma was his research student. He wanted to be among the new pioneers of psychedelic drug research and was about to embark on some kind of ayahuasca journey. Washington fell off my radar after the piece got killed and I never heard from Sharma again. That's probably why Leo had trouble placing the name. I must have mentioned it in passing once or twice. Oh, one thing I do remember about Sharma was a rumor that he got into some trouble for experimenting privately, but I don't have the details."

"Where is Clyde Washington right now?"

"I think he died, but I'm not sure. I could look into it."

"Yes, if you don't mind? And could you also check to see if he has a daughter named Wanda?" My mind races. Their use of psychedelics makes sense now. And, I'm beginning to see the connection between Wanda and Vikram—or Vincent—even clearer. That their ties go deeper than young love. Vikram grew up as Vincent on Salt Spring Island and had a relationship with Wanda and, through her, to Clyde Washington.

"Sure." Seb pauses, clears his throat. He knows better than to lie to me, but I sense he's hiding something when he asks how Leo is doing.

"Okay, I think. I'll ask him to give you a call when I see him."

Now is the time to ask about what's going on between them, but I have never pried into the particulars of their relationship before. The moment passes. Seb warns me to stay safe and says goodbye.

The thing is, he sounded as sad as Leo.

I've lingered here too long.

I don't know if Leo made it into this retreat or not. I didn't see his car outside but he could have parked elsewhere. If I knew for sure that he's not in the building, I'd leave the way I came in, but I can't get over the concern in Seb's voice. Leo could be drugged. He could need my help. I can't walk away.

There's a door from the main apartment that leads into the building. The door has been locked from the inside so when I exit the room I make sure to leave it unlocked. I pause in the hall, hear nothing, and continue on. There are five more doors on this floor. I listen carefully at each of them, but there is no indication that anyone is here. Which leaves the staircase. I take care to walk quietly, as quick and surefooted as Trevor in the forest. At the bottom of the stairs, I follow the sound of voices. Someone is crying and though every instinct in my body tells me to get as far away from this place as possible, I move toward the voices because Leo might be in there, tripping balls.

There's no way I'd leave him in the hands of some kind of mad scientist.

Down the hall, I come to a glassed-in studio and pull up short. The lights are dim but, from the hallway, I can still see inside. There are about eight people in the room. Leo isn't among them. Five people, including Cheyenne, are reclining on large mediation cushions and are in the throes of their own emotions.

Vikram and Wanda are here, too, observing the others so closely they don't even notice me. I step back into the shadows and think about what Seb has told me of the Wash Clinic and Hollywood House, with their supervised treatments that included counseling as well as dosing. The connection becomes clear now between Wanda, a trained psychologist and Vikram, said mad scientist. They may no longer be romantically involved but it's obvious they're still partners. They are both completely immersed in what's happening in the room, though Vikram is paying much closer attention to Cheyenne.

When Ken Barnes came into our office to talk about the case, he'd said that Cheyenne had struggled with depression during their marriage. Depression came up again in my earlier conversation with Gary's sister, who was concerned that he'd forgotten his medication.

I make another startling connection.

The doctor at the island hospital said a man was found to have taken ayahuasca—a potent hallucinogenic. Back when he'd been Vincent, Vikram Sharma had gone on some kind of ayahuasca journey.

What Cheyenne has found here is not only a lover, but also an unsanctioned, possibly illegal, treatment for her depression. Treatment through hallucinogenic experimentation. Possibly ayahuasca, but based on what was in the grow room, most likely psilocybin. The compound found in magic mushrooms.

This group of people came here for more than just

yoga. They came here to be treated. Dosed under supervision. This is an underground iteration of the Wash Clinic and what Spring Love has been hiding from the world. They are something of a cult, but one that even I hadn't expected. This is what they didn't want those workers to know anything about. What they couldn't risk any outsider seeing. But they couldn't keep this secret from Trevor.

Standing just off the studio, in the hallway, I take a quick succession of photos of the room and am about to back away when I nudge something on the wall, a small incense holder.

It crashes to the ground. Vikram looks up.

I don't know where Leo is, but it's a good thing he's not here because I've just run out of time. I head for the exit sign at the end of the hall, knowing that I've been seen by everyone in the studio, everyone in their right mind, at least, and maybe a few others who are not.

WHEN I GET outside, Trevor is nowhere to be found.

I call to him softly, but there's no response. Not even near the back stairs, where I saw him last. Now I know what put that look in his eye, and what makes him so angry at Vikram's presence in Cheyenne's life. He must have once crept through the apartment with the scarves and the hallucinogenic mushrooms, down the stairs, into the hallway, and seen the same thing that I did in the studio. His mother's depression treatment at work. And had no desire to see it again.

I don't blame him. It must have been an unsettling thing for a child to see, and I'm sure the courts would agree with me.

The lodge throws dim light into the darkness and, in this, I spot the point in the trees we'd emerged from. But when I go there, still no Trevor. I hear noises behind me, voices raised.

I dial Trevor's number. He doesn't answer. The voices get closer. Tucked just enough inside the woods to obscure the light from my phone, I hesitate briefly, then plunge in deeper. "Trevor," I call out. The crescent moon in the sky still sheds enough light for me to be seen if I'm not careful.

Trevor steps from the shadows, but won't meet my eyes. "Hey."

I go to him, but don't dare touch him. "You alright?"

"Yeah. Is my mom okay in there?"

"She is," I say. "Can you help me get out of here, Trevor?"

He frowns. "The quickest way is over here." He leads me deeper into the woods for a few minutes, then we emerge further down on that private road.

An engine revs somewhere back at the retreat. I motion for Trevor to follow me, then step into the tree line and go still.

The Spring Love pickup truck peels past us, sending a

spray of gravel and dust up into my eyes, but not before I catch a glimpse of Vikram in the driver's seat. Doesn't matter. I'm not afraid of Vikram. He can't poison me out here. He'd have to catch me first.

What I'm not prepared for is rustling behind us. Vikram has underestimated me, yes, but in turn I have underestimated Wanda, who is standing there with a double-barreled shotgun in her hands.

Chapter 11

MY HANDS GO up. I step in front of Trevor, partially shielding him with my body. He's gone silent, watchful. He could also be frozen at the sight of a weapon in front of him.

Wanda nods at Trevor, but addresses me. "His father sent you here?" I don't respond, which Wanda seems to take as an affirmative, because she continues. "You know, Cheyenne suspected it, but Vik and I told her she was imagining things. We thought you were a drifter, but that woman. I swear. Sometimes she has a sixth sense."

"Or maybe she's concerned about her kid. Maybe some part of her realizes what you all are doing in there isn't good for him."

Look at me, talking about motherhood like I know all about it.

Wanda doesn't buy my sudden expertise on the subject, either. "What we're doing is good for Trev because it's helping Cheyenne. She wants to get better for him. Do you know what it's like to go your whole life with people thinking your family is crazy?"

Yeah, actually. I know what it's like going my whole life thinking *my own* family is crazy. Based on what little I know of them. A mother who abandoned my sister and me, a father who died by suicide, a sister who pretends I don't exist and a daughter . . . well, I don't know her well enough to assess her mental health, but I'm not exactly hopeful at this point.

"I've heard of your dad," I say. "I don't think he was crazy."

This throws off her calm some. "He wasn't. Look, you might think you know what you saw in there, but you have no clue. My mom struggled with severe anxiety, even when she was working with my dad. She was his nurse, you know. They worked together to treat her, and others, too. People thinking their work was illegal, thinking it was wrong, it almost killed him. It did in the end, you know? After she died he experimented on himself because nobody would take a chance on his research anymore. He became . . . obsessed. His heart was bad and he still pushed himself. Vikram was there with him at the end. He was the only one who believed that what my dad was doing would help people."

"*You're* experimenting with people in there." And the reason Vikram might have gotten in trouble for his self-experiments as a young man is because he might have learned it from his mentor.

"No! You don't understand! This treatment works. It helps people. I won't let anyone take that away from us again." She glances from the camera around my neck to the space just behind me. "Come here, Trevor."

"Put the gun down first," I say. A shotgun is the kind of weapon with a big intimidation factor, that little old ladies use to scare away intruders and wildlife. It's not something that should be allowed near children and I sense that Trevor is as uncomfortable with Wanda as I am. Maybe it's the gun, or maybe it's her. Either way, it's not good. He hasn't said a word since Wanda showed up.

She doesn't listen. She opens her mouth and is about to speak when we are caught in the headlights of an approaching car. It's the Spring Love pickup, which has turned around. Wanda freezes. I stay where I am, too, because even though she doesn't seem particularly trigger happy, you never really know. The pickup stops in front of us. Vikram and Cheyenne approach, both shocked to see Trevor behind me.

"Trevor," says Cheyenne, a little unsteady. "Come here." Her pupils are dilated and her breathing is uneven. She's sweating, even though the night air is cool. Trevor stays put. "Trevor!"

Vikram steps in. "Wanda, put the gun down."

"Can people stop saying that? And I don't take orders from you, Vik," Wanda says, offended. She nods to me. "I just want to stop her. To make her listen so she won't ruin everything. We're helping people here and she doesn't understand. People don't understand! The patients that come to us, they're desperate."

"I know," says Cheyenne. "That was me, remember? Nobody can take away what you and Vik have done for people like me, but you know how I feel about violence. Please, you're scaring me."

Oh, I see. They don't like violence but poisoning someone is A-OK?

"You know who's desperate?" I ask, because I've recently been poisoned and can't stop myself. The teenage girl who shoved me comes to mind once more. I decide to forgive her. These people would drive anyone to violence. "Those workers you forced out because you were too scared of someone finding your little secret." I look at Cheyenne. "I thought Salt Spring Island had a history of being a place of refuge. But not for them, right?"

Cheyenne goes quiet.

"We paid them," Vikram says. "They were safe here."

"Please. You all had some romantic idea that you were helping these people but you sent them packing at the first sign of trouble. They don't matter."

This has clearly never occurred to them. There's a shocked silence that's broken by the sound of an engine, signaling the approach of another car. Still a ways off in the distance, but I can see it turn onto the gravel road we're on from the main road.

"Put the gun away before anyone sees," Vikram says. Sensible man. Or maybe he's the only one who's had a real run-in with the law, according to Seb, and is necessarily cautious.

Wanda nods at me. "We have to do something about her."

There's a tense moment. If they're going to do anything to me, they're going to do it now.

Vikram looks at Wanda and a silent message passes between them. She shifts her body weight, as if she's about to move.

"No!" Cheyenne cries, running to Trevor. She grabs him and pulls him away from me.

Vikram moves faster than I've ever seen him, away from me, though. He slides into the driver's seat of the pickup, reaches over and opens the passenger door. Then he motions to me. "Get in. Now." This time Wanda does point the gun at me, and keeps it trained until I'm inside. Then she gets into the backseat, scooting over to Vikram's side so she can keep watch on me through the gap between between the two front seats.

By the road, Cheyenne has her arms around Trevor. She is whispering to him, smoothing a hand over his cheek. He looks at me over her shoulder. I nod to him, to show him that I'm calm and that it's okay. He doesn't take his eyes off me as the pickup turns around and heads away from the retreat. When we pass the other car, Vikram flashes his high beams. There's a moment of extreme brightness and I see the other driver throw up an arm to shield his face. Vikram doesn't slow. Doesn't honk in apology. The peace-loving act he put on the first time we met has completely disappeared.

Now that Trevor isn't around, I'm thinking about that shotgun again. But we're in such close quarters that I can't afford to make any sudden movements, and I'm not sure that would be the best move in any case. I feel the tension rile up inside me, know this isn't a good thing. "Feels like old times, doesn't it?" I say to Wanda, reminding her of our trip to the hospital.

"Shut up and keep looking forward," Vikram says. Then: "So Ken sent you, eh? That bastard won't let Cheyenne be. Their marriage was the reason her depression got worse in the first place. Can't believe he's pulling shit like this."

I keep my mouth shut. I have no idea where we're going in the dark. There are no streetlights here, just the illumination thrown from the headlights showing a road hedged in by trees and blackberry bushes. We turn onto a dirt road. Vikram's pouty mouth is set in a thin line. Wanda's is, too, when I sneak a glance back at her. The road ends and just ahead of us is a great swath of moon-drenched sea. My guts clench in a moment of almost overpowering fear. The gun nudges into my right shoulder, sending a stab of pain through me. "Get out," says Wanda.

"Wait." Vikram reaches over pulls the camera off my neck. "You call the cops and we'll tell them you were a trespasser."

"I wonder what they'll say about the grow op at the yoga retreat."

"What grow op?" asks Wanda, her voice flat and hard. She nudges me with the gun. "This time don't come back."

I open the door and am halfway out of the truck before something occurs to me. I turn to Wanda. "Is that thing even loaded?"

"Of course it is," she lies. Then she jams the gun into my arm, pushing me off balance, half in, half out of the vehicle. Vikram puts the truck into reverse, tumbling me out for good, and backs onto the main road. I'm left sprawled in the dirt, stunned by the swiftness of it.

It takes me about five minutes to get off the dirt road and back to the main one, with the ocean behind me. I don't want to look at it now, at night with no one else around. There are no houses around here, nothing but a sliver of moonlight to guide me. I try to reach Leo a few times, but the calls go straight to voice mail.

There's a moment of inner struggle, then I call emergency services and tell them I think a child is in danger at Spring Love Farm, and that he has been exposed to hallucinogenic drugs. I don't feel better about it after I hang up, that sad, somewhat defeated look in Trevor's eyes heavy on my mind.

At least I don't have long to think about it. A car approaches, the same one that I'd seen coming down the gravel road at the yoga retreat. It stops in front of me.

Leo rolls down the window and sticks his head out.

"You alright, Nora? I thought I saw you in the passenger seat of that pickup but that goddamn hippie almost blinded me with his high beams."

When Vikram flashed his high beams and I saw Leo throw his arm up, I knew he'd come looking for me. "I'm fine. Did you see Cheyenne and Trevor when you drove up to the retreat?"

"Just now? No. Why?"

So Cheyenne must have pulled Trevor into the trees. I thought I'd seen that. "We have to get back to Spring Love," I say, as soon as I get into the car.

"Why? What did you find?"

I tell him about the grow op and the treatments. "Cheyenne's going to run with Trevor."

"Makes sense," Leo says, nodding. "That's probably why they drove you all the way out here, to buy themselves some time to get him away."

"If I was in her position, it's what I would do. In her mind, she's getting treatment for her condition, but from a court's perspective, she's experimenting with psychedelic drugs and there are drugs on the premises. It will go badly for her in the custody case unless she and Ken come to some kind of agreement." But it's Trevor who's on my mind, caught up in all this mess through no fault of his own.

"Can you prove it?" Leo asks.

"They took the camera you gave me." But I scroll though the photos on my phone, which I switched to in the grow room because the memory card in the digital camera was full. When Vikram pulled the camera off my neck, I let him because I knew the important photos weren't there. There's nothing a phone camera can't do these days. The pictures are incredibly detailed. Of the small-scale grow op, the lab equipment, the studio where Vikram and Wanda's "treatment" takes place.

"Can you go any faster?" I ask him, as he drives toward Spring Love.

"No, I'm having a tough time navigating these damn roads as it is. I spent most of my day getting lost, actually. When I got to the retreat they were immediately suspicious, but let me in the door because I said I heard about the place from Liz Rathburn. That's the only name I'd found online, of someone who'd actually been there. I had a little session with Wanda. She asked about the therapy I'd had in the past, and if I was on medication. She wanted detailed information about my mental-health issues and, after about twenty minutes, she kicked me out. Said she thought there'd be a cancellation but the last person showed up. I think she was trying to see if I really knew the Rathburn woman and decided I didn't."

"She probably didn't want to take any chances. Seb says you weren't answering your phone."

He shrugs. "I took a wrong turn getting here and running maps on my phone drained the battery, then I took a few videos of the property and recorded the interview with Wanda. By the time I got back to the car, my battery was dead and I left my charger back at the inn."

"I found it." That's why I wasn't too worried when I hadn't heard from him.

"We should call Ken Barnes," Leo says.

"He's not answering," I say, after several attempts.

We get lost twice on the dark roads while I try to reach Ken Barnes, so I stop calling him and use the map services on my phone instead. When we finally pull up to the yoga retreat, all the lights are off in the building and every single luxury vehicle that had been parked on the road is gone.

We drive to the main compound to look there, with no luck. There is no sign of Vikram, Wanda, Cheyenne, or Trevor.

They have disappeared—like the migrant workers they'd used to keep up the appearance of being a working farm—with a speed that astonishes both me and Leo. Which makes us realize they must have had yet another backup plan in place all along.

Chapter 12

KEN BARNES CALLS back before the authorities show up at Spring Love. I tell him to activate the GPS tracker he must have put on Trevor's phone. There's a brief pause but he doesn't deny that he keeps tabs on Trevor's whereabouts. What's the point of having children if you can't surveil them without their knowledge? "What's happened?" he asks finally. "And how did you know he has a phone? That's supposed to be a secret. I didn't want Cheyenne to take it away from him during one of her insane anti-technology rants."

I tell him I'll explain everything once he's located the phone.

When the police get to Spring Love, Leo takes over and sends me to sit in the car, citing my abrasive personality when dealing with authority figures.

Which is fair.

They find Vikram, Cheyenne, and Trevor heading toward the south point of the island in the Spring Love pickup. All that was left in the grow room at the retreat was the freezer full of mushrooms, left behind in haste. The other Spring Love hippies swear they don't know a thing about any of it and claim, with perfectly straight faces, that they have no idea where Wanda Washington is.

OUR FERRY THE next day is delayed. When we finally get on the damn thing, Leo is as exhausted as I am, even though no one has poisoned him, forced him into a vehicle at gunpoint and dumped him on a secluded road. Ken Barnes flew over on the seaplane this morning—a luxury that I would have gladly accepted if it had been offered to me. But such is not my luck.

Leo excuses himself to take a call but returns a few minutes later to hand me the phone. "It's for you," he says.

I take it from his hands. "Hello?"

"Hi," says Trevor.

"Hey. You with your dad?"

"Yeah."

"Where's your mom?"

"With Vik. She and my dad had a big fight and she's letting me spend the rest of the summer in Vancouver with him. She says I can take the guitar with me. I already asked her."

"Maybe you'll be an expert by the time you have to go back to school."

"Maybe," he says doubtfully. "Hey, what's your favorite guitar solo?"

"'Rumble.' By Link Wray. When it first came out it was banned on the radio because they thought it was too dangerous."

"How could it be dangerous?"

"Lots of people used to think music was dangerous because it makes you feel things that they sometimes don't like you to feel."

There's a pause on the other end of the line. "My mom feels things she sometimes doesn't like to feel," Trevor says, after a moment.

Shit. This isn't what I wanted. "I'm sorry," I say.

"It's okay."

I don't know what else to say, only Trevor is silent again and I really am sorry I made him feel that way. "Do you still have my number on your phone? The one your dad gave you?"

"Yeah."

"When you listen to 'Rumble,' send me a message and tell me if you think it's dangerous."

"Yeah?"

"Yeah. I'll be waiting for it."

We hang up after that. I hand the phone back to Leo. "Did Ken say what's going to happen to Cheyenne?"

"Well, the police are involved now but Ken says she's denying everything. When they picked her up last night, she claimed they were just going for a drive and they had all their stuff with them because they'd planned to go camping the next day."

"What about the photos I took?"

Leo rolls his eyes. "Apparently you walked in on one of their standard meditation sessions and she had no knowledge of a freezer upstairs. She told the police the room where they found the freezer was mostly Wanda's domain and she only ever used the studio to do yoga."

"Did they buy that? With Vikram's history?"

"No one has arrested either of them yet, so yes. I imagine so. But Ken has what he needs for the custody case, so our part is done."

After awhile I let it go, too. Quiet, solitary Trevor isn't my child. I don't know my child, only that, to the best of my knowledge, she's safe. Somewhere in Toronto, with her adoptive mother. Hopefully somewhere as accepting as Salt Spring was in the 1920s.

I keep thinking of that photo from 1929, of the schoolkids. It would be nice if the place where Bonnie grew up was as harmonious as Salt Spring Island once claimed to be. When I went looking for her, it turned something inside me. I think about her now, and worry about her environment, where before I never allowed myself to. In the quiet moments of the day, when I'm not busy at work, I walk with my dog and let my mind wander in her direction. Before she left for Toronto she hadn't wanted to see me. That's okay. I know she might never want a relationship. If I'm honest with myself, I wouldn't know how to start.

Leo seems to be in an odd mood today. We stand by the railing, Leo and I, and watch as the ferry pulls away from the harbor. I am looking for whales, as I've recently become obsessed with them. Leo is staring out into the distance, but I sense he has turned inward. Pensive. Absorbed with something I can't see.

As the ferry cuts through the ocean, heading toward Vancouver, I get a text from a Toronto number I don't recognize. It's a photo of a young woman's feet buried in sand, as water washes over her ankles. I've never seen these ankles before, but something about this photo arrests me. Then I realize it's not the picture itself. It's who must have sent it. I can't explain this feeling, but I know somehow this photo is from Bonnie, my estranged daughter. It's the first time since she's found out who I am that she's attempted to contact me. There are no words, but I really don't need them.

Suddenly, the sadness of the man at my side can't touch me.

Read on for an excerpt from the gripping
new thriller featuring Nora Watts

IT ALL FALLS DOWN

By Sheena Kamal

Chapter 1

WHEN THEY ERECTED their first pop-up tents to treat the addicts who wandered in and out like living corpses, I thought: Sure.

When the newspapers ran article after article about the opioid addiction taking the city by storm, it was more along the lines of, No kidding. Nothing slips past you guys.

But when the mental-health infrastructure became obsessed with the zombies, I had to put my foot down.

Nobody cared about my griping.

With all these people addicted to addicts now, where are the humble murderers of the city supposed to turn for our mental-health support? I ask you. We have been reduced to complaining about it in our weekly meetings. Not that there are murder support groups in Vancouver. I don't want you to get the wrong idea. Alternative outlets for the murderous of the city are sadly lacking. Private therapists can cost an arm and a leg—so to speak—and it's not like you can find community discussion groups on the topic, either. The closest I've found is one for people with eating disorders, but I don't expect people who have done terrible things to their appetites to understand that I killed a person or two last year. In self-defense, but still.

During my share, I settle for telling my fellow nutjobs that I feel like I'm being shadowed by my demons, and they nod in understanding. We are strangers who all know one another's deepest secrets, bonded in the sacred circle of a urine-stained meeting room in Vancouver's Downtown Eastside. They lift their anemic arms in polite applause afterward and we disperse from the collapsed circle. We are, blessedly, strangers again.

The feeling of being watched follows me from the low-income Eastside Vancouver neighborhood I frequent back to the swanky town house in Kitsilano that I now occupy some space in. I drive with the windows up because the air is thick with forest-fire smoke from Vancouver's north shore, smoke that has drifted here in pungent wafts and settled over the city. It doesn't help that we are experiencing one of these new Octobers that doesn't remember that there's supposed to be a fall season and is almost unbearably hot for this time of year.

As I drive, I obsess over still another death. One that hasn't occurred yet. But it will.

Soon.

Chapter 2

WHEN I GET back to the town house, Sebastian Crow, my old boss and new roomie, is asleep on the couch.

I reach out a hand to touch him, but pull back before my fingers brush his temple. I don't want to wake him. I want him to sleep like this forever. Peaceful. At ease. In a place where the C-word can't reach him. Every day he seems to shrink a bit more and his spirit grows bigger to compensate for the reduction of physical space he occupies. He's ill and there is nothing I can do about it because it's terminal. My dog, Whisper, and I have moved in to keep him company and make sure he doesn't fall down the stairs on our watch, but beyond that it is hopeless. There is a great fire that he seems to burn with now. His body has turned against him, but his mind refuses to let go just yet.

Not until the book is done.

When he asked me to help organize and fact-check it for him, I couldn't say no. Not to Sebastian Crow, the career journalist who is writing his memoirs as he nears the end of his life. Writing it as a love letter to his dead mother and an apology to his estranged son. Also as an explanation to the lover he has abandoned. What I have read of it is beautiful, but it means that he is spending his last days living in the past. Because there is no future, not for him.

Whisper nudges my hand. She is restless. On edge. She feels it, too.

I put her on a leash, because I don't trust her mood, and we walk to the park across the street. There's a man there who has been trying to pet her, so we steer clear of him in a spirit of generosity toward his limbs. On the other side of the park is a pathway that hugs the coastline. Smoke from unseen fires lingers, even here. Not even the sea breeze can dispel it. We walk, both of us feeling uneasy, until we circle back around to the park. I sit on a bench with Whisper pulled close.

The man who has been watching me walks right past us.

"Nice night for a bit of light stalking," I say. "Don't you think?"

The man stops. Faces me. He opens his mouth, perhaps considering a lie, but shuts it again. My back is to the dim streetlight that overlooks this section of the park. Whisper and I are just dark shapes to him, but he is fully illuminated. His coat is open and at his neck there is a long swath of mottled skin running from the hinge of his jaw to his collarbone. It looks like new skin tried to grow there once but gave up halfway, leaving behind an unfinished impression. He's an older man, but I find his age hard to place. Whatever it is, he has used his years to learn how to dress well. Sleek jacket. Nice shoes. It doesn't add up. A man, careful with his appearance, who spends his evenings sitting in a park and following women as they walk their dogs.

We wait in a kind of charged silence, all three of us. Whisper yawns and runs her tongue over her sharp canines to speed things along. He takes this as the threat it's no doubt meant to be.

"Your sister told me where to find you," he says finally.

If he thinks that's supposed to put me at ease, he's off his meds. Lorelei hasn't spoken to me since last year, since I stole her husband's car and ran it off the road and into a ravine.

But I decide to play the game anyway. "What do you want?"

"Damned if I know," he says, with a rueful smile. "Taking a trip down memory lane in my winter years, I suppose."

"And what's that got to do with me?"

"I knew your father once." It's a good thing his voice is soft, because said even a decibel louder, that statement could have knocked me on my ass, if I wasn't already on it. "May I sit down?" He gestures to the bench. There's something odd about his tone. His enunciation is too measured for someone confronted by an unpredictable animal. I wonder if the scar at his neck has anything to do with his casual demeanor. If he is one of those men who is so accustomed to danger that it doesn't faze him anymore.

"No. Knew my father from where?"

He pauses in his approach and considers Whisper's bared teeth. "Lebanon. You know he served with the marines there, right?"

I ignore this because I did not know that, but if it's anyone's business, it isn't his. "Doesn't explain why you're following me."

He swipes a hand over his face, the tips of his fingers pause at his scar. He notices my eyes flicker toward it. "From Lebanon. An explosion." He considers his next words carefully before he speaks. "I said I'd check up on you if anything ever happened to him."

I laugh. "You're a few decades too late."

"I'm not a very good friend. Look, I'm retired now and I had to make a trip to Canada. I thought I'd look you up. I had checked on you and your sister after I heard he died all those years ago, but you were with your aunt and everything seemed fine. A couple days ago I managed to track down your sister. She wasn't exactly very forthcoming about you—"

"She wouldn't be." Lorelei and I had not parted on good terms. She had kept her maiden name, though, when she got married, and had a robust online profile.

She wouldn't be hard to find, if you had a mind to go looking.

"I told her we were old friends. Took some convincing, but she told me that I could find you through Sebastian Crow. And here I am."

"But why?"

He becomes agitated, fishes out a lone cigarette from his jacket, and lights it. His eyes linger on the wisp of flame from the lighter. "You ever made a promise you didn't keep? I've done a lot of wrong in my life, but how things turned out with your father, in the end . . . I never thought what happened to him was right. I knew he was struggling after the trouble in Lebanon, but goddamn. What a waste."

He looks down at my hand, where my fingers are clenched so tight around Whisper's leash that my nails dig into my palm, leaving crescent-shaped marks.

"I don't know what I'm doing here," he says helplessly. He hasn't taken a drag of the cigarette yet, seems to have no intention of smoking it.

I almost drowned last year. I don't remember a lot about it, only that I must have blacked out at some point. Any free diver or scuba enthusiast will tell you that in the final stage of nitrogen narcosis, latent hypoxia hits the brain. It can cause neurological impairment. Reasoning and judgment are often affected, at least in the moment. But it can also feel pleasant, this lack of oxygen. Warm. Safe, even.

It can make you delusional.

I wonder if I'm experiencing a more long-term fall-out from my near drowning. Because I used to be able to tell when people were lying, almost definitively. But now I'm not so sure. After the events of last year, when my daughter went missing—the girl I'd given away without a second thought—I have looked at people differently. Maybe it's my sluggish maternal instincts kicking in, muddling my senses. Or maybe I've lost my mojo. Because when he said he doesn't know what he's doing here, I believed him. I believe that we do things that don't make sense. Even to ourselves.

It's also possible that I am falling into my own hallucinations.

I'm so confused that I say nothing at all in return. The veteran looks as unsettled as I feel. I stare at him hard until he walks away, toward the ocean, and disappears into the dense night. Then I rub some feeling back into my hands. My thoughts are a jumble, until one of them shakes loose.

It isn't just the surprise of someone coming to find me after all these years. It isn't even that he felt the need to follow me in the dark to ascertain whether I'm doing okay. It goes deeper than that, and has to do with the things about my father that I don't know. That there was trouble in Lebanon. With my father.

My father had trouble in Lebanon, and then, some years later, he blew his brains out.

Chapter 3

DEEP IN SPACE, a star named KIC 8462852 flickers for some unknown reason, while down on Earth an ex-cop, ex–security agent, ex-husband, and ex–amateur bowler grimaces as he downs a glass of spinach juice and hopes that his internal organs are paying attention to the effort he's making on their behalf.

This particular star has confounded scientists the world over by its constant dimming and brightening, while Jon Brazuca confounds only himself with his new resolution to be kinder to his body. He inherited low self-esteem from his spineless mother and weak-chinned father, both of whom apologized through life and then on into their retirement.

But Brazuca is over it. This demeaning cycle of "I'm sorry" and "I beg your pardon" would end with him.

He is turning over a new leaf, and then blending it into a smoothie.

The evening sun is low on the horizon and he is filled with chlorophyll and contentment. Brazuca has always been more awake at night, more alive, and has now turned to astronomy to help fill in the gaps. He is not a man of science but wishes that he were. His mother had once taken him to Spain as a child, to the cliffs of Famara, and together they had looked out at the stars reflected in pools of water on the beachfront below.

Thinking of this, he longs for a simpler time, when women he generously pleasured didn't drug him and tie him to a bed, leaving him to be found by astonished maids. Which is something that actually happened to him approximately a year ago. Nora Watts, the woman he'd attended AA meetings with, the woman who had gone and lost a daughter that she hadn't even wanted, the woman whom he felt compelled to help for no rhyme or reason that made any goddamn sense to him—she had left him high, literally, but not at all dry. No, she'd fed him a booze-and-sedative cocktail that put him to sleep and gave his body the little bump it had been wanting for so very long.

And it has taken him months to kick the habit again.

Brazuca stands on the balcony of his apartment in East Vancouver and winks up at the sky, in the general direction of the flickering star he has read about in a magazine. He feels for a brief moment a sort of affinity for the universe. He chugs the rest of the juice and belches in contentment.

His friend Bernard Lam has asked him to come over and, for the first time ever, he feels like hanging out with a billionaire.

"BRAZUCA," SAYS LAM, at the door of his sprawling Point Grey mansion. If there's a housing crisis in Vancouver, it might be because so much space has been taken up by this single estate. There's an east wing and a west wing, and about twenty rooms in between them. There are outdoor courts for every sport, and a miniature golf course for variety. If you get bored of the saltwater pool, there's a freshwater one on the other side of the property.

Bernard Lam, the playboy son of a wealthy businessman and philanthropist, gestures for Brazuca to follow him inside. His famous charm is nowhere to be seen. His manner is grave and uncertain as he leads Brazuca down a long hallway filled with family photographs mounted on the wall, newer photos of Lam and his recent bride, and then into a study. "What's wrong?" Brazuca asks as soon as the door is closed behind them.

"One moment." Lam goes to his laptop on the desk. There's a bottle of scotch next to him and no photos to speak of here. It is a family-free zone. Lam turns the screen toward Brazuca.

"She's beautiful," he says, glancing at the woman on Lam's computer. In the picture, she's in a sundress on a yacht, laughing up at the camera. She's tall and voluptuous, with a sheet of glossy dark hair and bright eyes.

"Her name was Clementine. She was the love of my life."

No amount of spinach juice can stop the headache that begins at Brazuca's temples at Lam's use of past tense. The woman in the photo wasn't the woman on the walls of the family home. So the love of his life was not Lam's new bride. "When?"

"They found her last week in her apartment. They say it was an overdose. She's . . . she *was* four months pregnant."

"Yours?" Brazuca asks, careful to keep his voice even. Lam raises a brow, as if the possibility of anything else doesn't even exist.

Brazuca decides not to push. "So what do you need?"

"You're still working with that small PI outfit? They give you any time off?"

"I take contracts as needed. They're flexible." His new employers weren't picky about what work he chose, as long as he took some of it off their hands. They'd even offered to make him a partner in a more formal sort of arrangement, but he'd said no to that. He didn't want formal.

"Good," says Lam. "That's very good. I need you to find out who her dealer is."

"Bernard . . ."

"You will, of course, be generously compensated."

"It's not about the money."

"Then do it for a friend. Do it for me. My girl and my child are dead. I want to know who's responsible."

Brazuca wonders if Lam knows that, with the use of the word *girl*, he has painted both of them with the same brush of idealized innocence. "You're not going to like what comes out of this," he says quietly. "It will bring you no peace of mind." Death by overdose is a nasty thing to deal with. Blame is hard to pin down.

"Who says I want peace of mind?" Lam pours a shot of scotch into his glass and knocks it back. "I'll give you the paperwork and her contacts. They didn't find anything on her phone. The drug she took . . ." He looks away, gathers his thoughts. "It was cocaine laced with a new synthetic opiate now hitting the streets. A fentanyl derivative more potent than what's been seen before, and actually stronger than fentanyl. Called YLD Ten."

"Wild Ten? I've heard of it. Not much. But I know it's out there." It was the stupid name that got to him. Easy to remember when you place an order from your friendly neighborhood drug dealer.

"Then you know how dangerous it is. She was only twenty-five. She had her whole life ahead of her, Jon, and it was with me. I need to know. Please."

"Okay," Brazuca says, after a minute. Because he's not the kind of man who can say no to a cry for help. Turns out, his leaf isn't so fresh after all. "I'll look into it. Do you have a key to her apartment?"

Lam nods. "Of course. I own the place."

"Of course," Brazuca murmurs. "I'll get started right away." He doesn't have to say the "sir" because it's implied. Bernard Lam, whose life he saved several years earlier, is oblivious to this dig.

Acknowledgments

I SPENT A few months on Salt Spring Island, back when I'd first moved to the west coast. During the time I lived there, I had no idea it had such a rich cultural history.

Liberties were taken in describing certain aspects of the island, naturally, but the photograph Nora sees in the archives is real and is included in a book by Evelyn C. White called *Every Goodbye Ain't Gone: A Photo Narrative of Black Heritage on Salt Spring Island*.

British Columbia does have an interesting history with psychedelic drug research, which may be seeing something of a resurgence. I am indebted to Travis Lupick for his reporting on this subject in the *Georgia Straight*.

About the Author

SHEENA KAMAL holds an HBA in Political Science from the University of Toronto. She was awarded a TD Canada Trust scholarship for community leadership and activism around the issue of homelessness, and has worked as a researcher into crime and investigative journalism for the film and television industry. Her debut novel, *The Lost Ones,* was inspired by her experience. She lives in Vancouver, Canada.

Facebook: /SheenaKamalAuthor
Instagram: @sheenakamalwrites

Discover great offers, exclusive offers, and more at hc.com.